There was an envelope that said, "To Val to Be Read on Her Eighteenth Birthday." There was over a year to go before her eighteenth birthday. Over a year where her whole life could change. Her mother hadn't wanted her to know what was in that envelope for another whole year and more. To open it now would be to disobey the last request her mother had made of her. It would be an act of disobedience Val could never be forgiven for.

She opened the envelope carefully, as though leaving it in one piece would make what she was doing less wrong. She took out the sheets of paper and left them folded for a moment. She didn't have to read what they said. She could wait until she was eighteen, or until morning, or burn them. She opened the letter.

Other Bantam Starfire Books you will enjoy

Most

Precious

Blood

· · ·

Susan Beth Pfeffer

BANTAM BOOKS

NEW YORK · TORONTO · LONDON · SYDNEY · AUCKLAND

MOST PRECIOUS BLOOD

A Bantam Book

PUBLISHING HISTORY
Bantam hardcover edition published September 1991
Bantam paperback edition / April 1993

The Starfire Logo is a registered trademark of Bantam Books,
a division of Bantam Doubleday Dell Publishing Group, Inc.
Registered in U.S. Patent and Trademark Office and elsewhere.

ISBN 0-553-56128-6

Bantam Books are published by Bantam Books, a division of Bantam
Doubleday Dell Publishing Group, Inc. Its trademark, consisting of the
words "Bantam Books" and the portrayal of a rooster, is Registered in
U.S. Patent and Trademark Office and in other countries. Marca
Registrada. Bantam Books, 666 Fifth Avenue, New York, New York
10103.

PRINTED IN THE UNITED STATES OF AMERICA

RAD   0 9 8 7 6 5 4 3 2

Most Precious Blood

. . .

Chapter 1

• • •

OF COURSE THERE was background. Words as angry as the ones pouring out of Michelle's mouth didn't emerge without some sort of history behind them. Val reminded herself of that in the locker room as she tied the laces of her running shoes. Or did she mean to untie them? It was hard to concentrate.

She tried untying her laces to see if that felt better. Whatever she was supposed to do, she was glad to have a reason to be looking down. Michelle was standing right in front of her. Val could feel the words flow down on her like mud.

"You broke your promise again. You always do. You just do what you want, and the hell with everybody else."

Val's back was starting to hurt from the stooping. She didn't know how much longer she could continue to tie and untie and tie again. At some point she would have to look up and confront her cousin's angry eyes.

"You're so spoiled, Val. You always have been. You've always been given everything you want. You expect the world to revolve around you."

"You've made your point already, Michelle," Kit Farrell

said. "Before school and during lunch and now here. Give it up already."

Michelle whirled to face Kit. "The mouthpiece speaks," she said. "The defender of the faith. Like father, like daughter, right, Kit? I hope your retainer is as big as your father's."

Val used the moment to sit up straight. "Stop it," she said. "If you're angry at me, don't take it out on Kit."

"It's all right," Kit said. Val knew Kit meant it, but she didn't care. Michelle had never liked Kit, had always resented Val and Kit's friendship. Michelle wanted desperately for Val to like her as much as she liked Kit. It wasn't that Val failed to understand Michelle. That wasn't part of the background.

"Is that where you were?" Michelle asked. "Did you decide to spend the day with precious Kit instead of coming over to my house? Did you think you'd have more fun running wild with her than having a family dinner? One my mother worried about for days, and you never showed up."

"I told you I was sorry," Val said. She sighed. It was Monday, and the dinner had been scheduled for Sunday afternoon. Knowing Terry, Michelle's mother, she probably had worried for days. Terry worried about everything, but especially about pleasing Val and her father. Neither one of whom came for dinner. "Daddy had to go out of town on business. And I had that paper to write for English. I'd forgotten all about it, and you know what Sister Gina Marie is like when you don't hand a paper in on time." It was a lie, and they both knew it. Val simply hadn't wanted to have dinner with Michelle's family. Not given the tension that currently existed between their fathers. Tension that Val suspected Terry had hoped to dissipate with a Sunday dinner.

"Is that why you didn't answer the phone all day?" Michelle persisted. "You were so busy working on your paper you didn't even hear it?"

Val nodded. Another lie. She didn't answer the phone because she was a coward. Because she'd been hoping to avoid the wrath she was now facing.

"Are you sure you weren't at Kit's instead?" Michelle said. "Enjoying yourselves, making fun of me and my mother? Getting drunk with her mother instead."

A direct hit. Val looked anxiously at her friend to see how she would take it. Kit's mother's drinking was one of those things everybody at school knew about, but most of them were too polite or frightened to mention. Not Michelle when she was angry. For Michelle there were no barriers of decency.

"My mother isn't getting drunk this week," Kit said. "We took her to a rehab center yesterday. You're a jerk, you know that, Michelle."

"So that's where you were," Michelle said. "Spending the afternoon driving up to some posh joint for lushes in Connecticut probably. You thought that was more fun than having dinner with my family, didn't you, Val? You thought Kit's mother was more important than mine."

Val stood up. She carefully folded her gym clothes and put them in her book bag. "I'm sorry about dinner yesterday," she said. "I'll call your mother as soon as I get home and apologize to her. Now will you drop it, Michelle?"

But Michelle wasn't about to drop anything. It wasn't her nature to. Val remembered an incident when the girls were ten, when she and Michelle were supposed to go into the city for the day with their mothers, and she'd had to cancel because of a toothache. Michelle still brought that one up on a regular basis. Val was almost surprised Michelle hadn't mentioned it already.

"She cried," Michelle said. "You made my mother cry. Do you like that, Val? Does that make you feel good?"

"I said I was sorry," Val declared. Terry cried easily. At Val's mother's funeral, Terry's weeping drowned out everyone else's sorrow. In some dark murky way, Val had never forgiven her those sobs. They seemed cheap and theatrical. Of course that had been over two years ago, and Val knew she shouldn't bear a grudge. That was Michelle's specialty.

"We're going to be late for English," Kit said. "Come on, Val." She took Val's arm and began leading her out of the locker room.

Val looked around. The other girls had already left. They must have sensed the best part of the fight was over. It probably peaked for them with Michelle's comment about Kit's mother. Or maybe they'd left even before then. Val couldn't remember when she'd last noticed the other girls. She hoped for Kit's sake they hadn't overheard everything.

She felt a moment of petty satisfaction when she handed in her paper to Sister Gina Marie. She'd finished the paper days earlier, hadn't even looked at it yesterday, but at least it was done, and Michelle couldn't know exactly when it was finished. Michelle handed hers in as well, but Kit didn't.

"I'm sorry," Kit said. "Something came up this weekend. I'll hand it in tomorrow."

"Yeah," Michelle whispered. "They had to bail her mother out of the drunk tank."

The girls sitting around Michelle tittered. Val knew Kit must have heard, but she didn't say anything. She just stood there, making eye contact with Sister Gina Marie. Val had gone to Most Precious Blood with Kit, and Michelle for that matter, since kindergarten. She'd seen Kit stare straight at teachers, even the nuns, while clearly defying them for years now. But she never quite got over her feeling of admiration. When Val was in trouble, she always looked down.

"All right," Sister Gina Maria said. "See to it you hand in the paper tomorrow, Kit."

"That's not fair," Michelle said. "How come Kit gets an extension like that, and none of the rest of us do?"

"None of the rest of you asked for one," Sister Gina Marie replied.

"That's because you said no extensions," Michelle said. " 'No extensions, no exceptions.' You said that on Tuesday when you gave us the assignment. And now you've made an exception. And Kit didn't even give a reason. You didn't even ask for one. That's not fair."

"You're right," Sister Gina Marie said. "It is unfair. You're all juniors in high school now. I think it's time that you learned life is unfair."

"But Michelle's right," Jennifer Riccio said. "You did say no exceptions, and now you made one for Kit. I had a busy week too. I didn't want to waste my time writing some stupid paper for you, but I did. And Kit didn't, and she's getting away with it."

"I haven't read your paper yet, Jennifer," Sister Gina Marie said. "But when I do, I'll be sure to keep your opinion of it in mind. If you think it's stupid, then undoubtedly it is."

Kit had sat down. Val thought she saw a glimmer of a smile on her face. They both liked Sister Gina Marie, who'd only been teaching at their school for a couple of years. She hadn't calcified yet. Sometimes they even heard her laugh when she talked with the other teachers.

"I still don't understand why you're letting Kit get away with it," Michelle said. "We all had to give up things to write our papers. Val was supposed to have dinner with my family, and she had to cancel just to write her paper. Why does everybody treat Kit like she's queen around here? It's been going on for years now. Kit always comes in number one. She always gets the best grades. Everybody always likes her best. It's unfair, and I'm sick of it."

"This is an English class," Sister Gina Marie said. "Not a TV talk show. If you have any differences with Kit, I suggest you discuss them after school. We have our own work to concentrate on today."

For a moment, Val thought Michelle wouldn't stop. She could be like that, get wound up over something and not be able to let it go. Val felt pity for her cousin, pity and affection and concern. And guilt. Michelle would be fine if she'd only showed up for dinner. And Kit would have been spared a couple of embarrassing scenes as well. Val wished she could go back in time just a day, so she could endure the occasion she'd avoided. So what if Terry got weepy, as she undoubtedly would have, simply because Val's father hadn't come too. So what if Bob, Michelle's father, had cast dark and angry looks at her. Whatever was going on was between Val's father and him, and had nothing to do with Val. Her father always kept his business dealings from her. And whatever was going on between her father and his cousin Bob was business. A deal, Val suspected, that Bob had assumed he'd get a share of and didn't. Bob always took Val's father's business dealings personally.

It would have been one lousy dinner to sit through,

tears and anger and noise from Michelle's kid brothers and foolishness from her older sister, but Val was used to that. She even envied it sometimes. She was an only child, and she wished for brothers and sisters, especially in the years of her mother's illness. Things had been so quiet then. Things were never quiet at Michelle's house.

Kit had an older brother, Kevin, but he was five years older, and ignored the girls. He was at Notre Dame now. Last summer he went to Europe. The summer before he'd had a different excuse. There'd been another boy in between, but he'd died when Kit was just a baby. Val looked around the classroom. They all had backgrounds, she realized. Each of them had a family history that influenced everything about them. Even Sister Gina Marie, although it was hard to think of a nun, even a young one, coming from a real family. Kit claimed nuns were hatched, like chickens. Val smiled.

"Do you see some humor in Juliet's plight that escapes me, Val?" Sister Gina Marie asked. "If you do, I wish you'd share it with us."

Val shook her head. "I'm sorry," she said. "I was thinking of something else."

"You all seem to be thinking of something else today," Sister Gina Marie declared. "Don't you think October is a little early for spring fever?"

The girls laughed. Val was glad for the excuse to laugh with them. It relieved some of the tension.

"Very well," Sister Gina Marie said. "Since none of you seems willing to think about *Romeo and Juliet* right now, perhaps a surprise quiz might make you focus on your work."

The protests were immediate and loud. "A quiz? That's not fair. I was concentrating. Will it count in our averages?"

"A quiz," Sister Gina Marie said. "And of course it will count in your averages. If I'm going to have to grade them, the grades should have some meaning. Take a sheet of loose-leaf paper, and I want each of you to take one member of the Montague family and one of the Capulets, and write about how each of them felt about the feud, quoting from the play. Don't use either Romeo or Juliet, it has to be other family members. This is an open-book quiz. Now get to work, and try to remember your grammar and spelling in this hour of need. All right. You may begin."

The girls opened their copies of the play and searched frantically, trying to find family members and references to the feud. Val searched along with them, but her mind still was on her own family. Bob was angry at her father. Michelle was angry at her. Terry and Kit were innocent bystanders caught in the crossfire. So was Sister Gina Marie for that matter, and now all of them who had to take a surprise quiz suffered as well. Just because Bob thought his cousin Rick, Val's father, had cut him out of a deal. This was definitely carrying the sins of the father too far.

Val noticed Kit beginning to write. She was always the first and the best. Val envied her friend her intelligence almost as much as she envied her her courage. She envied Michelle her family, and Jennifer Riccio her endless stream of boyfriends from their brother school, Sacred Heart. She envied everybody who wasn't in Sister Gina Marie's English class just then.

All that envy wasn't getting the quiz done though, so Val bent over, looked at the play, and began to write. She didn't find much to say about the feud, but she quoted Shakespeare liberally and hoped for the best, much the same way, she suspected, everyone else in class was doing.

Sister Gina Marie told them to hand in their papers moments before the final bell rang. Val sighed with relief at the signaling of the end of the school day. It had been a killer, one she was glad had finally ended. Now a quick trip to her locker to get her jacket, and then Bruno would drive her home. Her father was still gone, not expected back before Tuesday, maybe even Wednesday, but she didn't care. Maybe she'd call up Kit once they were safely home, and invite her over. Or maybe Kit could convince her father to take them both out for supper. They ate out a lot whenever Kit's mother was away. And Kit's father, being Val's father's lawyer, would know that Val was alone for the night. Val knew this rehab trip must have been an emergency, Kit hadn't mentioned it at all the previous week, but that didn't mean Val wouldn't be welcome for dinner. She wouldn't ask while they were in school, since that would just get Michelle started all over again, but afterwards she would call. She was sure they'd be willing to let her come over, maybe even spend the night. Val realized then how little she wanted to be alone in her house. Not really alone, since Bruno and his wife, Connie, would be there. Val was never left alone, not even to go to and from school. But she'd feel alone anyway, with her father gone. No matter what shape the Farrells were in, it would be better than being alone.

"I hope you're satisfied," Michelle said as Val made her way to her locker. "That pop quiz was all your fault."

"I know," Val said. "I was the one who got on Sister Gina Marie's nerves by badmouthing Kit."

"Kit gets away with murder," Michelle said. "She probably aced that quiz. And I'll flunk it, and so will half the other girls. And I was only mad at Kit because of you, so it is all your fault."

"Will you stop it already," Val said. "I've apologized twenty times for skipping dinner. It's not the end of the world, you know."

"My parents had a huge fight because of it," Michelle said. "Mama wouldn't stop crying and Dad belted her one."

"I'm sorry," Val said, feeling even more uncomfortable. "I really am." She looked down at her shoes and saw she was still wearing her running shoes. She must have forgotten to take them off in the locker room. She was relieved none of the nuns had seen, since sneakers weren't allowed in the classrooms.

"You could come for supper tonight," Michelle said. "Mama would be so glad if you did. She told me to ask you."

Val pictured the evening: screaming kids, Terry with a black eye or a cut lip. That was one of the things her father held against Bob, that he smacked his wife around. A real man never hit a woman, not according to Val's father. He had other ways of gaining her respect.

"I can't," Val said. "I promised Daddy I'd stay in this evening."

"This is all your father's doing," Michelle said. "Has he told you not to have anything to do with me? Is that it?"

"Of course not," Val said.

"You're lying," Michelle said. "Daddy said last night that Rick wouldn't let you come. He said Rick must have forbidden you to have anything to do with us because he knows he did a wrong thing not letting Daddy into that apartment complex he's building in Teaneck. Daddy says whenever Rick cuts him out of a deal like that he always acts like we're not really family, like family doesn't really count."

"Dad didn't even mention it to me," Val said. "The only reason I didn't go to dinner with your family was because I didn't want to. That's all. It wasn't because of Dad or Kit or anybody except me. I didn't want your mother crying on me, and your father giving me dirty looks. I'm sorry. I should have gone, but I didn't. All right?"

"I knew that was it," Michelle said. "I knew you were just being stupid and selfish and spoiled. You didn't want, so you didn't bother. You've never thought about another human being in your life, Val Castaladi. It's always just me, me, me."

Val stood still. She knew her best chance was letting Michelle get all of it out of her system. Most of the other girls had left already, but she could see Kit lingering by her locker. Kit had always protected her. Val couldn't see asking her to stop just then.

"You're spoiled and you're selfish," Michelle said. "I remember even when you were little, you always had your own way. Mama says when you were a baby, if you even just whimpered, your mother would pick you up and give you anything you wanted. She said she always knew you would turn out bad, the way you were spoiled and your heredity and all. And she was right. You're going to end up in big trouble one of these days, and that precious father of yours won't even bother to bail you out. That's when you'll see blood counts for something."

"What the hell are you talking about?" Val asked. She knew if she pushed harder, horrible things would be said that could never be taken back. But she was tired and angry, and it had been a long lousy day, with Michelle carping at her since before the first bell, and she wanted it finished already. "Are you accusing my father of something? If you are, just say it."

"So you can leap to his defense, the way you always do?" Michelle asked. "I don't see why you bother. It isn't like he really is your father."

Val slapped her. It was an instinctive reaction, and she knew then just how Bob must feel, and she knew she would never forget that feeling and always hate herself for it.

Michelle stood absolutely still, then rubbed her cheek with her hand. "It's true," she said. "And it's about time you knew it. He isn't your father. Everybody in the family knows. I'll bet even Kit knows. Probably half the girls in school know too."

"Stop it, Michelle!" Kit said. She hadn't moved any closer to the girls, and Val took that to be an ominous sign. Why wasn't Kit by her side, protecting her with more than distant words? What was Michelle saying, and how could it possibly be true?

"Everybody knows except you," Michelle said. "It isn't like something like that can be kept secret. If you weren't so dumb and so spoiled, you would have realized it long ago. You're not really family. You don't really count."

"You're a liar," Val said, praying that that was true. Holy Jesus, make her a liar. She couldn't even look down any more, she was so afraid the ground beneath her was cracking.

"Don't say any more," Kit said. Had she edged any nearer? Val couldn't be sure. "Michelle, stop, before you regret it."

"Of course you would know," Michelle said. "Your father must have done all the legal work. Assuming Rick bothered making it legal. If jail wasn't involved, he probably didn't care."

They were on safer ground now. "Dad's never been in jail," Val said. "Your father's been, but not Daddy."

"Daddy," Michelle mocked her. "You can't call him that. Not when he isn't even a relative of yours. Unless of course you are. Maybe you're his bastard, and he just brought you home for your poor mother to raise as her own. Maybe all those times she picked you up and cuddled you, she was hoping you would die. Maybe it was hating you that killed her."

Val leaned against the wall of lockers. Michelle was speaking loudly enough that she had gotten the attention of everybody still in that wing of the school. Sister Gina Marie stuck her head out of her classroom. "Stop this at once, Michelle," she said. "Or you'll be in big trouble."

"I won't," Michelle said. "Val's sixteen. She's old enough to know."

"Know what?" Val cried.

"You really are stupid," Michelle said. "You're adopted, you bitch. You're no more a Castaladi than Kit is."

Chapter 2

· · ·

THE COMBINATION LOCK cut into the small of Val's back. She thought, I'll be paralyzed. The rest of the world seemed to be already. Michelle, Kit, even Sister Gina Marie, were all standing absolutely still, frozen at the moment of truth and betrayal.

Val sensed she was the only one who could force them out of their poses. "Liar!" she cried. The word worked. Michelle gasped, then ran down the hallway. They could hear the click of her heels against the floor and the stairs, could hear her open the door, could imagine hearing her running off the school property, to her home, to her bedroom, to her own private corner of space. And once there was no more Michelle, Kit and Sister Gina Marie came alive. They rushed over to Val, who wasn't sure whether the wall was holding her up, or she holding it, but feared the consequences of moving away from it as much as she'd ever feared anything, even her mother's death. Sister Gina Marie looked as though she wanted to do something, to reach out to Val, but then she pulled back. Kit didn't hesitate. She grabbed Val's arm and pulled her toward the center of the hall.

"Sit down," she said. "Put your head between your knees. I think you're going to faint."

Val did as Kit told her. Kit had a bossy streak. It was something Val had put up with all the many years of their friendship. At some point, Val would have to complain to Kit about it. But at that moment, it felt better to do as Kit told her, to have the blood rush back into her head, to feel less woozy, more in control.

"Can you believe her?" she asked. "Saying things like that?"

Neither Kit nor Sister Gina Marie answered. Val didn't know what to make of their silence.

She tried standing up, and found with a little effort she could force her legs into place. Standing up was good. She could look straight at Kit and Sister Gina Marie. "I've seen her angry before," she said. "Michelle has a terrible temper. She gets it from her father." She remembered hitting Michelle and felt weak again. Her father had never hit her mother, never hit her. Her mother, even when she was strong and healthy, had never hit her. Yet she'd seen them both angry, had provoked their anger on more than one occasion. They must be saints, she thought, to keep from hitting.

"She was lying," Val said. "I didn't know Michelle lied, but she was real angry, and I guess that's why. I hope she doesn't keep lying. I'd hate it if she kept lying like that, lying about me. She can lie about herself for all I care, lie about anything she wants to, except me. Me and my family, that is. She should never lie about family. How could she say something like that? She has to know it isn't true. Her father and my father are cousins. Her name isn't Castaladi like mine, but she's one anyway. I can't remember a time when I didn't know Michelle. She gets mad all the time, and she's a very jealous person, but she's never lied before. Why do you think she's lying now?"

"I think we should get the school nurse," Sister Gina Marie said, but she didn't move.

"I don't need a nurse," Val said, and then realized she was going to have to prove it. "I'm fine."

"Bruno must be outside," Kit said. "Bruno is the Castaladi chauffeur. He takes Val to and from school. He can drive Val straight home."

"No," Val said. "I don't want to go home." She surprised herself with the words, and with how deeply she meant them.

"All right," Kit said. "You'll come home with me."

Val nodded. She bent down, gathered her books and her jacket, which seemed to have fallen onto the floor, and straightened herself out. It wasn't hard to put on her jacket, to stuff her book bag with books. It wasn't even hard to look straight at Sister Gina Marie. "I'm fine, really," she said. "Michelle and I will work it out. Don't report her or anything, all right."

"I'm not worried about Michelle," Sister Gina Marie replied sharply. "I'm worried about you."

"I'll take care of her," Kit said. "It'll be all right." She smiled at Sister Gina Marie, then taking Val by the hand, led her down the corridor. Val could sense Sister Gina Marie looking at them, but it didn't matter. The important thing was to get out of there, and not to go home.

"I'll tell Bruno he's taking us to my house," Kit said, once they were outside. Outside felt good. The crisp October air refreshed Val.

"No," she replied. "Don't bother with Bruno. I want to walk."

"I'll tell Bruno that then," Kit said.

"No!" Val said. "Don't tell Bruno anything. I don't owe him any explanations. He isn't my jailor. If I want to walk home with my friend, then I'm just going to walk home with my friend. Everybody else does it, just walks home, no chauffeur to drive what, half a mile, maybe less. Let's just walk."

"Stand here," Kit said. "Don't move." She used her best no-nonsense tone, and Val obeyed her. She watched as Kit deliberately disregarded her wishes and walked to the car, stuck her head in, and told Bruno what Val's plans were. Val couldn't understand why people treated her that way. Didn't her wishes count for anything?

"I told you not to do that," she said to Kit as the girls began their walk off the school grounds.

"I heard you," Kit said. "But you were wrong. Bruno had been waiting there for ten minutes already. He was worried. If you'd just walked off without saying anything to him, he would have followed us to my house to make sure you were okay. I told him you stayed late because you had to talk to one of your teachers, and that you were coming to my house to have supper with my father and me. Now he won't worry, and he won't call your father. I did the right thing."

"You did the smart thing," Val said.

"Yeah," Kit said. "That's what I'm good at. The smart thing."

"You're not going to get your paper done," Val said. "The one for Sister Gina Marie. You won't get it done tonight, will you."

Kit grinned. "It'll keep," she said.

"I've never just done something," Val said. "I've never just gone over to your house, or stayed late after school, or gone to the mall without telling anyone I was going.

Bruno's always known, or Connie. You do things by your-self all the time, don't you. Take walks, visit me, shop. You don't have to report to . . ." She paused for a mo-ment, trying to find the right word to label Bruno and Connie. Servants didn't sound right. They were family too, some distant cousins of her mother. Her mother and Connie had gone to school together. Saint Ursula Ele-mentary and Our Lady of Lourdes High School in Queens. They called her father Ricky, the way her mother had. Servants didn't do that. Even Jamey Farrell, Kit's father, called her father Rick, and Jamey was Rick's best friend.

"My father doesn't worry about me the way Rick wor-ries about you," Kit replied. "He worries about my mother instead."

"But that's my point," Val said. Until that moment, she hadn't realized she had a point, so she got even more excited. "Worrying doesn't help. It doesn't stop anything."

"It stops you from going to the mall," Kit replied.

Val nodded, and when she did, she discovered that moving her head unleashed a terrible headache. "This has been the worst day of my life," she declared. "Even worse than the day they told me how sick Mama was."

Kit stopped walking. "Then you believed her?" she asked.

"No, of course not," Val replied. "Michelle was lying. Why should I believe her?"

"I don't know," Kit said. "It just seems to me if all you think it is is lies, this shouldn't be the worst day of your life."

"I think I flunked that pop quiz," Val said. "And I have a headache. And it makes me really angry that I can't just walk to my best friend's house without having to report in to my . . ."

"Bodyguard," Kit said.

Val turned sharply to face her friend. Her head nearly exploded from the gesture. "He isn't my bodyguard," she said. "I don't have a bodyguard. I don't need a bodyguard. What made you say something so stupid?"

Kit shrugged her shoulders. "This hasn't exactly been my best day either," she declared. "Better than yesterday maybe, but not by much. I'm sorry if calling Bruno a bodyguard offends you."

"Daddy's a businessman," Val said. "Businessmen don't need bodyguards. At least not for their daughters."

"I guess not," Kit said.

Val's brain eased itself back into her skull. She could feel the wretched pain subside. "How bad was it?" she asked. "This weekend."

"You don't want to hear about it," Kit replied.

"I do," Val said. "Really."

Kit smiled. "Then I don't want to talk about it," she said.

"Was she very drunk?" Val asked. It would be good for Kit to talk. She kept too much locked in. Jamey was like that also, but her father said that was good in a lawyer. It wasn't necessarily good in a sixteen-year-old though.

"Yes," Kit said. "She was." She paused for a moment, but Val kept on walking. She didn't think her head could take another sudden stop. Kit stared at her, then scurried to catch up. "I meant to write the paper," she said. "I like Sister Gina Marie. I didn't want to put her on the spot like that."

"What would you have done if she refused to let you hand in the paper late?" Val asked. Papers seemed like such a pleasant subject, compared to the alternatives.

"I wouldn't have promised to write the paper," Kit said. "I would have taken the F instead."

"You never got an F in anything," Val declared. "You've always talked your way out of bad grades."

"This one wasn't that important to me," Kit replied.

"What would Jamey have said?" Val asked. "If you brought home an F."

"It's hard to say," Kit replied. "He might have gotten angry. Or maybe he would have understood. Pop isn't always predictable."

"You're the only person I know who calls her father Pop," Val said. "Pop. I like it. Maybe I should call Daddy Pop."

"Don't," Kit said. "It would be too confusing. Besides, Rick is hardly a Pop."

"Neither's Jamey," Val replied. She laughed. They were two blocks from Kit's house, and she was starting to block out everything that had happened in school that day. She loved October. It was her favorite month. She remembered suddenly a perfect October Sunday from years before, she must have been around nine, when out of nowhere her father suggested that he and Val's mother and Val all go to the Giants football game. Neither Val nor her mother had ever been to a game before, and they spent a wonderful hour just debating what to wear, finally settling on brand-new wool skirts, and cashmere sweaters of blue and green. Bruno had driven them, but Val didn't remember him at the game. She didn't have that many memories of just her parents and herself, with nobody else along. The afternoon was sunny and perfect, the seats were on the fifty-yard line, and Val was cocooned between her mother and her father, blanketed by her parents' love for each other and for her. During half time the three of them stood on line together to get food and souvenirs, and Val could still feel the warmth of their hands as each one held one of hers. Her father had promised her mother that if the Giants won, she could buy a new fur coat, and the Giants did, so on the drive home all her mother did was joke about how expensive the coat was going to be. She and Connie went shopping for it the very next day. Silver fox, still sitting in a closet. Val supposed it was hers now. Whenever her mother wore it, she called it her football souvenir, and Val's father always laughed and said that was the last game he was taking them to, it was too expensive a proposition.

Val was glad October was her favorite month. May used to be, but her mother died in May, and she couldn't shake off the associations. Of course the way her head felt just then, she couldn't shake anything off. She laughed again.

"I'm going to have to call Pop," Kit said. "Tell him that you're here. He didn't want anybody over today. We were going to spend the evening just straightening things out."

"What things?" Val asked.

"It was a bad weekend," Kit said. "There's a lot of breakage. We got in too late last night to do anything about it."

"What if all that business with Michelle hadn't happened?" Val asked. "Would you have invited me over anyway?"

Kit shook her head. "Not tonight," she said. "I would have just cleaned up what I could and made omelets for Pop and me and written that paper for English."

It bothered Val that she wouldn't have been welcome at the Farrell house that night. They knew her father was away, how lonely she could get with just Bruno and Connie around. Her head throbbed. She knew she could never forgive Michelle her lies. Was Kit turning on her too? "What if I'd insisted?" she asked. "What would you have done then?"

Kit thought for a moment. "I would have called Pop and told him not to come home from the office," she replied. "Then I would have made you help me clean up. I may make you do that anyway. Do you think you can be trusted around broken glass?"

"Of course I can be," Val said. "What are you so worried about? I know Michelle was lying. I'm not adopted. How could I possibly be adopted?"

Kit shifted her schoolbag so she could examine her bitten-off fingernails.

"I'm not adopted," Val said.

"We'll discuss it inside," Kit replied. She unlocked their front door. "The living room is okay. Most of the damage is in the kitchen, and their bedroom."

Val loved Kit's home. Her own was Tudor, old fashioned and dark. Kit's house was bright and airy. Jamey collected contemporary art. Their walls were covered with boldly colored paintings.

"Oh, no," Kit said, walking over to one of them. "Mother slashed this one. She must have done it with this." She gingerly picked up a piece of broken glass and sighed. "It's one of Pop's favorites too. I'd better call Pop and tell him you're here."

"I'm sorry," Val said. "I shouldn't have come." She hadn't realized it until she saw the way the canvas had been ripped. She didn't belong there any more than she belonged at home. At that moment, there was nowhere she belonged, but that was hardly Kit's responsibility.

"It's all right," Kit said. "You're here, you might as well stay. I'll worry less if I know where you are. Sit down. I'll call Pop from the den."

But Val wasn't ready to sit. She walked around the living room making an inventory of damaged goods. Then she walked to the kitchen. It was a nightmare of spilled and spoilt and broken. She found a box of garbage bags, pulled one out, and started filling it with things that could never be repaired.

"Thank you," Kit said when she saw what Val was doing.

"She must have gone on a rampage," Val said. "Couldn't Jamey stop her?"

"He wasn't here for most of it," Kit said. "Neither was I, for that matter. I got here first, but you know, she's bigger than I am, and I couldn't talk her down. I got to the den and I called Pop, and he came right over, but by then the worst was over. He was at the office." She began picking up shards of glass and dropping them into the opened garbage bag. "She destroyed some things in my room too," she said. "Not much, but she's never done that before. I guess because I wasn't home. I didn't tell Pop. I don't know. Maybe I should."

Val tried to remember her own mother, but all she could picture was how she looked in her coffin. "This has really been a lousy day," she said. "I'm sorry. I'm not making things any better for you and Jamey."

"You're wrong," Kit said. "You're a distraction. Besides, you're helping clean up. The more we do, the less Pop'll have to." She bent over and picked up a bowl. "Damn," she said. "Mother likes this one. She'll be upset she broke it."

"Maybe you can glue it back together," Val said. "Do you have all the pieces?"

Kit shook her head. "It isn't worth it," she replied. "Mother broke it once already. Maybe she doesn't like it after all. I always thought she did."

Val opened up another garbage bag and started putting broken egg shells in it. "Do you love her?" she asked.

"Oh, yeah," Kit said. "More often than not. You loved your mother, after all, and she spent years being sick."

"It wasn't her fault," Val said. "She didn't ask to get cancer."

"I know," Kit said. "But you resented it anyway."

Val sat down on a kitchen chair, making sure first that there was nothing broken on it. "Michelle was lying," she said. "She had to have been."

Kit continued picking up broken pieces of china. Her back was to Val. "Are you that sure?" she asked.

"All right," Val said. "What do you know?"

Kit continued to look away. "I don't know anything. It's just I have a funny feeling about it."

"Look at me," Val said. "Please."

Kit turned around and faced her.

"What do you mean by a funny feeling?" Val asked.

"It's hard to explain," Kit said. "You know how sometimes you hear something and you didn't know it, but you feel like you know it already?"

"No," Val said.

"Yes, you do," Kit said. "It was like that for you when they finally told you your mother had cancer. You knew something was wrong, but they kept denying it, and you wouldn't admit it to yourself either, but you knew, only you didn't. And then they told you."

"I knew she was sick," Val said. "I just didn't know with what."

"You knew something was the matter," Kit said. "But you didn't know she was sick. Don't forget, I was around. I was the one you talked to. You thought your parents were thinking about a divorce. That was the only thing you could think of to make them whisper."

"So I was wrong," Val said. "But I had my suspicions. Are you going to tell me you've always suspected I was adopted?"

"I've wondered," Kit said. She picked up an empty orange juice carton and threw it into the garbage bag, then got a sponge, and began wiping the dried-up juice off the counter.

"What was there to wonder about?" Val asked.

"Why you're an only child," Kit said. "Why you don't have any brothers."

"Mama was sick," Val said.

"Not until you were ten," Kit replied. "Almost eleven. And your parents were married for a long time before you were born. What was it, seven, eight years? That's eighteen years for your mother to give your father a son. You don't think Rick wants a son to carry on the family name?"

"Maybe Mama miscarried," Val said. "Like Connie. You know how hard she and Bruno have tried having kids, and they've never managed."

Kit nodded. "That's one of the things I've remembered," she said. "Mother was talking to Pop about it once, years ago. About how Connie wanted to go to some shrine to pray for safe delivery for her babies, and your mother wanted to go with her. Mother thought that was barbaric, making a pilgrimage. She's never really gotten the hang of Catholicism."

"But that doesn't mean I'm adopted," Val said. "Suppose Mama did want to go with Connie. It could mean she wanted to have more babies, to give Daddy a son, and she was miscarrying or having trouble conceiving, and she thought going to the shrine could help. That's all."

"It just seems like a funny thing for Michelle to lie about," Kit said. "And you said it yourself. She doesn't lie. That's half her problem, the way she hangs onto the truth and uses it over and over again. If she just lied, everything could be forgotten."

"Your mother sure made a mess of things," Val said. "Can you really clean it up by yourself?"

"I'll do what I can," Kit said. "The main problem's my bedroom. She hacked at my mattress with some scissors. I don't know how I can get a new one without telling Pop."

"How can you stand it?" Val asked.

"I need a new mattress anyway," Kit said. "The old one was getting lumpy."

"I'm not adopted," Val said.

Kit rinsed out the sponge. "I think you'd better stop saying that," she declared. "And really think about it."

"There's nothing to think about," Val said. "If I were adopted, they'd have told me. Nobody keeps that kind of thing a secret anymore. Caroline O'Mara's adopted, and she's always known. That was practically the first thing she told people in kindergarten, that she was adopted."

"Caroline O'Mara's parents are different from yours," Kit said.

"And what's that supposed to mean?" Val asked.

Kit started scrubbing egg yolk off the window. "It doesn't mean anything," she said. "It means everybody's parents are different from everybody else's. Caroline's mother probably doesn't have drunken fits where she smashes up the entire house. Your mother never did either. She got sick and died. Caroline's mother plays golf. My father still thinks he's going to write a novel someday. Your father likes to go sailing. Everybody's different. Everybody handles things differently."

"You really think Michelle was telling the truth?" Val asked.

Kit nodded.

"You're wrong," Val said. "And I don't want to stay here any longer."

"All right," Kit said. "Call Bruno and tell him to pick you up."

"I will not," Val said. "I'm perfectly capable of walking home on my own."

Kit put down the sponge. "I'll walk you home then," she said.

"Why are you treating me like such a baby?" Val asked.

"Because you're behaving like one," Kit replied. "You know you aren't allowed out alone. Now it's either Bruno or me, or you stay here. Those are your choices."

"No," Val said. "Those are Daddy's choices. Mine is to walk home by myself, and that's what I intend to do."

"Fine," Kit said. "If Bruno isn't your bodyguard, I'm certainly not. Thank you for helping me clean."

"You're welcome," Val said. She stormed out of the kitchen to the living room, where she got her book bag and her jacket. The torn canvas of the painting flapped its farewell.

Chapter 3

• • •

FIVE BLOCKS AWAY from Kit's, Val spotted Bruno driving the car toward her. Kit must have called him the moment she left, Val thought. She used what remained of her will power not to stop, and kept on walking, as Bruno drove just past her. He used a driveway to make a U-turn, then followed her the ten or so blocks home.

Connie was waiting at the door for her. "I have cookies," she said. "Fresh baked. Want some?"

"Not right now," Val replied. Bruno and Connie had to know something was up, but not even Connie would think the disaster Val was in could be salvaged by cookies. "I have a headache. I'm going to my room."

"Michelle called," Connie said. "I told her you were at Kit's."

"Thank you," Val said. She could just imagine what Michelle had to say. Probably that her parents were Siamese twins, and she'd been adopted out of the circus. She walked upstairs to her bedroom, closed the door, and threw herself on her bed. She shouldn't have. Her head began throbbing again.

The phone rang. It was Val's private line, so she knew the call was for her. In spite of that, she picked it up.

"Are you all right?" Kit asked.

"I'm fine," Val said. "You didn't have to send for Bruno."

"You didn't have to leave," Kit replied. "Do you want to come back? The kitchen's pretty much done."

"Some other time," Val said. "Thanks anyway."

"I'm sorry," Kit said. "I'll see you in school tomorrow?"

Val realized that was a question. It hadn't occurred to her to skip school. "Of course you will," she said.

"Okay," Kit said. "Oh, Michelle called here a few minutes ago. I told her you were on your way back home."

"Thanks," Val said. Apparently, there would be no avoiding Michelle. She hung up the phone, and rested on her bed. She loved her bedroom. Right after her mother died, her father had agreed to let her redecorate, and it was the only space in the world Val thought of as being truly her own. The walls were lavender, the woodwork and curtains crisp and white, and the bedspread she currently lay on lavender and purple flowers. Her mother had hated lavender. "It's an old lady's color," she'd said once. When Val had picked lavender for the walls, she'd felt naughty and rebellious and just a little bit guilty all at the same time.

She could picture her mother now, in the quiet darkness of her bedroom, not just in illness and death, but the way she'd been when she'd been healthy as well. Val had loved her mother, who seemed always willing to play dolls with her, or school, or dress up. "Don't tell Daddy," her mother used to say when the two of them would share a forbidden activity, putting on makeup, or going to the movies. Val smiled at that memory. Her mother would tell Bruno to drive them to Terry's house and pick them up there in three hours, and once they were safely dropped off, the two of them would run the five blocks to the local movie theater and see a movie instead. Bruno never suspected a thing, or if he did, he never let on. Her mother loved to laugh. That was how Val knew things were bad before anybody told her. Her mother didn't seem to laugh anymore.

The telephone rang. Val told herself not to answer it, but picked it up anyway. Michelle would just keep calling until they spoke.

But it wasn't Michelle. "Hi, honey," her father said. "Just thought I'd see how you're doing."

"I'm fine, Daddy," Val said. "How's Washington?"

"Lousy," her father replied. "Same as always. They're real song-and-dance men over at HUD. Half of them tell you one thing, the other half say just the opposite."

"Sounds bad," Val said. She forced herself to sit up, and was surprised by the wave of nausea the motion evoked.

"I've had better days," her father said. "And you?"

Val laughed. "I've had better ones too," she replied.

"Anything the matter?" her father asked.

"I skipped dinner yesterday at Terry's, and Michelle was real mad at me," Val said. "And we had a pop quiz in English I think I flunked."

"Sounds like a perfect Monday, all right," her father said. "Tell you what. Next weekend, if the weather's any good, let's go sailing. We may not have another chance before springtime. We'll make a day of it. Sailing in the afternoon, dinner out someplace nice. What do you say?"

"That sounds great," Val said. "I'd like that a lot."

"Tomorrow, after school, tell Bruno to take you and Connie shopping," her father said. "Buy yourself a pretty dress. You can wear it Saturday night. And a nice sweater or two. You'll need one for sailing."

"Thanks, Daddy," Val said. "I'll model them for you tomorrow."

Her father was silent for a moment. "I don't think I'll be making it back tomorrow," he said. "Probably Wednesday instead."

Val wasn't sure whether she was disappointed or relieved.

"I guess if you and Michelle are on the outs, you wouldn't want to stay there," her father said. "How about at the Farrells? They're always happy to have you."

"Amanda Farrell's in a clinic again," Val said. "They took her to one yesterday."

"That's okay," her father said. "Kit'll be grateful for the company. And I'd just as soon not have you spend time there when Amanda's drinking. Why don't you have Bruno drive you over now, and you can spend the next couple of days there. Connie can take both you girls shopping. Tell Kit to buy herself something pretty, my treat."

"I think I'll stay home tonight, Daddy," Val said. "I have kind of a headache. But maybe tomorrow I'll stay with Kit."

"I don't like the idea of you being alone for so long," her father said. "Is it a bad headache? Do you want Connie to call the doctor?"

Val managed to laugh. "It's nothing serious," she said. "I'll take a couple of aspirin, it'll go away."

"If it doesn't, you have Connie call the doctor," her father said. "No matter how late. Promise?"

"I promise," Val said.

"I'll try to make it home tomorrow," her father said. "I can't make any guarantees though."

"I'll be fine by tomorrow," Val said. "Surprise quizzes give me headaches, that's all."

"Do you want Kit to come over and keep you company?" her father asked. "I can call and tell her to."

"Kit has a paper she has to write," Val replied. "She didn't get it done over the weekend, and Sister Gina Marie gave her a one-day extension. I think we'd better leave her alone to finish it."

"Tea's good for a headache," her father said. "Tell Connie to make you some tea."

"I will," Val said.

"I'll call you in the morning before school to make sure you're okay," her father said. "And if you need me for anything, Connie has my number here. All right?"

"I'm fine, Daddy," Val said. "I won't be needing you."

Her father laughed. "I'm not sure I like the way that sounds," he said. "But you don't feel well, so I won't argue with you. Take it easy tonight. Don't worry about homework. You can catch up tomorrow when you're feeling better."

"I'll see you on Wednesday," Val said.

"I'll talk to you tomorrow," her father replied. "And think about shopping. That always used to cure your mother's headaches."

Val hung up the phone and rested her head against the pillow. She hated going shopping with Connie, who had no taste whatsoever. It was more fun to go with Amanda, who could be scathing if she or Kit picked out something really wrong, but who had a great eye for just what would look good and could even explain why. But Amanda was out of action for the next few weeks.

The telephone rang again. Val grinned. She was never so popular as when she wanted to be left alone. She picked it up, said hello, and waited to hear Michelle's anguished or angered voice.

But it wasn't Michelle. "Val?" the voice said instead. "This is Sister Gina Marie."

Val sat up, her back absolutely straight, the way the sisters always taught them. "Yes, Sister," she said.

"I'm just calling to see how you are," Sister Gina Marie declared. "You must have been quite upset after that scene today."

"I'm okay," Val said.

"I called you at Kit's, but she said you'd gone home. Is your father home? Have you had a chance to talk with him?"

"He's in Washington," Val said. "He just called."

"Did you discuss what had happened with him?" Sister Gina Marie asked.

"No, of course not," Val said, starting to feel annoyed. Most Precious Blood was a small, expensive school, and it prided itself on its teachers' involvement with students, but this was carrying things too far.

"Do you think . . ." Sister Gina Marie began. "Well, maybe it would be best for you and your father to talk about it in person."

"There's nothing for my father and me to talk about," Val declared. "Goodbye, Sister." She hung up the phone before Sister Gina Marie had a chance to protest. What business was it of hers? She'd just happened to overhear Michelle's lies, that's all. And now she was acting like they were true.

Val continued to sit up. The room was dark, but she could see the framed photograph of her and her mother she kept on her dresser. If Michelle hadn't been lying, then there might be something about it in the school records. Maybe Sister Gina Marie had looked up her file and read that she was adopted, and that's why she called.

Maybe all the teachers knew, had known for years, since Val had started school there, and none of them had told her.

The phone rang again. Val's thoughts were so upsetting she was willing to speak to anyone, even Michelle. So she answered.

This time it was Michelle. "Are you okay?" she asked.

"I'm fine," Val said. She was getting tired of having to tell people that.

"I've been trying to reach you forever," Michelle said. "First you weren't home and then you weren't at Kit's, and then the phone's been busy. I thought maybe you took it off the hook so you wouldn't have to talk to me."

Val instantly regretted not having thought of that. "It's okay," she said.

"I just wanted to apologize," Michelle said. "For being mad at you all day and being so bitchy, and then for what I said."

"I should have had dinner with you last night," Val said. "That was my fault."

"Then you forgive me?" Michelle asked.

"Sure," Val said. "Why not."

"Well," Michelle said. "I mean, I shouldn't have said all those things."

"You were angry," Val said. She didn't understand why she had to absolve Michelle, but Michelle certainly seemed to expect it.

"I was," Michelle said. "But I still should have kept my mouth shut about the adoption."

"It was a stupid lie," Val said.

"It wasn't a lie," Michelle said. "Are you accusing me of being a liar? I've never lied about anything in my life!"

Val hung up the phone before Michelle's shrill voice

pained her any more. When the phone rang again, she didn't answer, and then she took it off the hook. For a moment it buzzed its annoyance, and then it was silent.

This is foolish, Val told herself, and she turned on the light by her bed. It took her eyes a moment to adjust, but even though the light made her head throb, she kept it on. What difference did it make that Michelle was sticking to her ridiculous story, that Kit believed her, that Sister Gina Marie was concerned? Val knew herself. She knew her parents. She could hear the love in her father's voice when he spoke to her on the phone. She could remember how she and her mother had giggled together when they snuck off to the movies. Caroline O'Mara's mother never giggled. She just played golf.

If she had been adopted, Val decided, her mother would have told her. Maybe not when she was little, but at some point. Her mother wouldn't have just died without telling her, or at least hinting. Her mother loved her too much not to have given her some warning.

Val got up and walked over to her closet. She pulled out the lavender-flowered hatbox she'd requested for her fifteenth birthday, and opened it. Inside were all her favorite, most secret possessions. With a sigh, she took out the notebook her mother's nurse had given her three months before her mother's death.

"Write things down," the nurse had said. "You may find that helps."

Nothing had helped during those months, and Val was never much of a writer anyway. But when a grownup told her to do something, she did it, so there were two months worth of entries. Val hadn't touched the notebook since the day of the funeral. It wasn't a period in her life she ever wanted to relive. But maybe her mother had said something, and she had been too young or too scared to realize what she'd meant.

The entries started out long and flowery, as though Val had expected the sisters to grade her work. But within a couple of weeks they were short, half-finished sentences. "Bad night." "Mama very sick." "Heard Daddy crying."

It hurt Val to read those entries, but she skimmed through anyway. Close to the end of her notations, she found what she was hoping she wouldn't.

"Mama says she wrote me letter."

Val closed her eyes and tried to remember the conversation. Her mother had been given a lot of drugs, and she wasn't always coherent, and Val had been a little scared of being alone with her. But this was one of the better days. "I wrote you a letter," her mother had said. "But don't open it now."

Val had promised not to, then changed the subject. There had been so much she'd wanted to tell her mother in those last weeks, not important things, but the sorts of things they'd always talked about, friends and school and family. Her mother had loved those conversations, and Val had tried to come up with funny stories to entertain her and make her laugh. So Val knew then and now that the letter was something her mother judged serious. And Val knew the time had come to find the letter and read it.

She left her bedroom and went to her mother's room. Her parents had shared a bedroom until the last few months of her mother's illness, and then her father had moved into one of the guest rooms, and ended up staying there. So her parents' room remained pretty much as it was during her mother's life. Val couldn't remember the last time her father had gone in there.

She walked to her mother's closet, opened the door, and

looked for the old shoe-box her mother had cherished. "My wedding shoes came in this box," she'd told Val when Val was very little. "So I keep all my favorite, most secret things in it. Daddy just thinks it has shoes." She and Val had giggled that Mama could put one over on Daddy, who was so smart about everything. Once or twice her mother had taken the box out to show Val her treasures. There were photographs of old boyfriends in there, and one of Val's father looking very young and foolish in a bathing suit. There were letters Val's uncle had written before he'd been killed, and a pressed corsage that gave everything in the box the faint scent of gardenias. There were a couple of pieces of junk jewelry, whose significance Val could only guess at, and a lock of baby hair she knew must have been hers. And there was an envelope that said, "To Val to Be Read on Her Eighteenth Birthday."

Val took the letter out. She sat on the floor by the closet and thought about disobeying her mother. She couldn't remember many times when she'd willfully disobeyed either of her parents. There had never seemed the need. Sure they had rules, and their rules could be strict, but they were her parents, and you always did what your parents told you. After her mother's death, there seemed to be fewer rules. She didn't have to be quiet anymore, and for a while her father didn't even seem to care if she did her homework. She did it anyway. It gave her something else to think about.

There was over a year to go before her eighteenth birthday. Over a year where her whole life could change. Her mother hadn't wanted her to know what was in that envelope for another whole year and more. To open it now would be to disobey the last request her mother had made of her. It would be an act of disobedience Val could never be forgiven for.

She opened the envelope carefully, as though leaving it in one piece would make what she was doing less wrong. She took out the sheets of paper and left them folded for a moment. She didn't have to read what they said. She could wait until she was eighteen, or until morning, or burn them. She could call her father in Washington and tell him what Michelle had said. She could go back to Kit's and talk with her about mothers. She opened the letter.

My Darling Valentina,

Today is a good day, and I can sit up in my chair. The sun is shining, and I can see the first daffodils blooming in the garden. I do not know how many more good days I will have, so although I dread writing this letter, I am making myself do it now.

Many times when I lie in my bed I think about you and what your future will be like. You are such a pretty girl, I know that many boys will fall in love with you. As you read this letter, you are eighteen. Perhaps you are already in love. Perhaps you are even married. I was engaged to your father when I was eighteen. We married when I was nineteen and two months old. Your father was twenty-six. He knew much more of the world than I did, but he was always a loving and gentle man, and I cannot picture my life without him. I pray that someday you will also know this sort of love.

I come from such a large family, two boys, four girls, and your father also comes from a family with brothers and sisters. Your father's oldest brother took over their father's business. His next brother died. And your father, with his father's help, went into business for himself, and made his fortune building houses and apartments. I wish you had known your grandfather better. He was always so proud of Ricky.

My family and Ricky's family had done business together, and everybody thought we would make a fine match. I had always thought him so handsome, and was thrilled when he asked me to marry him. We waited until after I graduated high school, and then there were some problems, so we were engaged a long time.

I know you've seen the pictures from our wedding, but it was even more beautiful than that. I had four flower girls and six bridesmaids and Terry was my matron of honor. I would have asked my sister Angie, but she was seven months pregnant with your cousin Mike. My friend Rose Vitelli caught my bouquet, and six months later she got married.

Your father and I were happy as newlyweds, although we were much teased about when we would have our first baby. But months turned into years, and no matter how we tried, I was never able to become pregnant. I am sure by now the sisters have taught you how babies are made, but sometimes no matter how much a husband and a wife love each other, they cannot create a life together. That was how it was for Ricky and me. After five years, we went to doctors and had tests done. What their results were, I don't really know. My heart was breaking from not having babies. I would see my sisters and my cousins always with babies and my arms were empty and I was filled with sadness.

Your father knew how much I hurt, and he hurt too, since he dreamed of a son who would take over his business someday, the way his older brother had taken over their father's. Sometimes I was afraid that Ricky would leave me for a new wife, one who could give him children, but he always swore he loved me and would never leave me. I said many prayers. Only my cousin Connie, who was not barren, but could not bring a child to full term, knew the pain I felt.

Then one spring day your father placed a baby in my arms and said here is the daughter you've dreamed of for so long. I could not believe the gift. You were the most perfect baby I'd ever seen. Your father said that you were six weeks old and that I could name you whatever I wanted, since you were too young to know what your name was. Six weeks earlier had been Valentine's Day, so I named you Valentina. My family teased me because it was such an old-fashioned name, so we called you Val. I loved you from the moment I first held you in my arms. It never mattered to me that you were not from my womb. You were my daughter, my precious Valentina.

At first your father didn't seem to care much about you. I knew he was still sad that he could never have a son. But one day you crawled to him and lifted your arms up for a hug, and he picked you up and embraced you and from that day on, I know that he too loved you as much as if you'd been his own.

I never wanted you to know you were adopted, but now I am so sick and I worry that you will worry you'll inherit cancer from me. They say it runs in families. Perhaps you wish to marry, but you are afraid to, because you know how much your father has suffered from my illness. And that is why I'm telling you this. Of course I do not know what your real family was like, *but mine has always been sickly and two of my sisters died before they were sixteen. You have always had excellent health, and the doctors have told me there is nothing to worry about for you. They say you should live to be an old woman surrounded by your grandchildren, and they told me this even before I became sick, so it wasn't just words to cheer a dying woman.*

I wish I could be there on your wedding day. I wish I could see your children and grandchildren, hold them in my arms as I once held you. I know that you and your children will bring much joy to Ricky and that makes me glad when my heart is filled with such sorrow.

My darling Valentina, you have always been my daughter, and I will watch over you from heaven and protect you with my love.

> *With love and kisses,*
> *Your mother*

Val folded the letter and put it back in its envelope. She returned the envelope to the shoe-box, and the shoe-box to its rightful place in the closet. She closed the closet door, turned off the light in what had been her parents' bedroom, and walked back to her own room. She crossed over to her bed, sat down on it, and before she began crying, she pictured plunging a knife into her mattress and ripping it and everything else she had once thought of as hers into shreds.

Chapter 4

• • •

I T WAS HARD eating breakfast the next morning under Connie's watchful eye. It was hard reassuring her father over the telephone that the headache was gone. It was hard following the regular pattern of getting into the car with Bruno. But Val did all that, and everything else that was required of her, to escape the house on Tuesday.

She knew one slip and everyone would know something was wrong. She hadn't eaten dinner the night before, so breakfast was a necessity. Otherwise Connie would call her father, and he'd come home early. She knew if she revealed anything through her voice or her manner on the phone, her father would know something was wrong, and come home early. She knew that Bruno was already troubled by her actions, and even the smallest sign of rebellion would alarm him sufficiently to tell Connie, if not her father. Knowing all that made it easier for Val to act as though everything were normal. She couldn't bear the thought of Bruno and Connie, both of whom had known all along about the deception, but even more than she hated them, she dreaded the idea of seeing her father.

Rick, she thought to herself, as Bruno made the short

drive to school. He isn't my father at all. He's just some man named Rick.

Unless he was her father, and he had foisted his bastard child on Val's mother to raise. But wouldn't her mother have guessed? There was nothing in the letter to suggest that possibility, just how much she loved her husband, how grateful she was that he hadn't left her for someone who could give him children.

But if he wasn't her father, how had he gotten her? Where did she come from?

Kit met Val at the car door. "You'd better be prepared," she whispered as Bruno drove off. "Everyone's talking about you."

"About me?" Val asked. This was a nightmare she hadn't anticipated.

"A couple of the girls must have heard Michelle yesterday," Kit replied. "Five of them have already asked me if it's true. About the adoption, I mean. Most of the others edged over to hear my answer."

Val felt sick to her stomach. "I can't go in," she said.

"Do you want to go back home?" Kit asked.

Val shook her head. "I can't go there either," she said. "Give me a moment. I'll be okay." She stood absolutely still, then took a deep breath.

"They won't bother you," Kit said. "They won't come up to you or anything. But you were bound to overhear, so I wanted you to be prepared."

Val remembered what it had been like the days after her mother had died. Half the girls had been overly concerned, the other half had avoided her. Right then, she favored avoidance.

"What did you tell them?" she asked, suddenly curious about how Kit had handled things.

"I told them Michelle was jealous because Larry DeVito asked you out and not her," Kit replied.

"But that's a lie," Val said. "He never asked either of us out."

"I know," Kit said, looking smug. "But they're not about to run over to Sacred Heart to ask him. And it gets the gossip running in a whole different direction."

"You are Jamey's daughter," Val said, and then those very words pained her. A spasm shook her body, and she buckled over.

Kit grabbed her fast and blocked her from the other girls' view. "Can you go through with this?" she asked.

"I have to," Val said, straightening up. "I'm sorry. I'm feeling kind of lost right now."

"What happened?" Kit asked. "Did your father say something?"

"My mother," Val whispered. "She left me a letter. It's all true."

The first bell rang. "I'm sorry," Kit said. "I was hoping it wasn't."

"You and me both," Val said. "Come on. I'll talk to you later."

Kit nodded. She and Val walked into the school building together. Val was aware of all the eyes on them, and that made her just angry enough to stand tall and walk at an appropriate pace. She spotted Michelle in the school yard as they approached the door, but neither one said anything. Michelle didn't look so great herself. Val hoped she was being plagued with questions about Larry DeVito, a boy who Michelle had had a crush on for going on two years.

The morning wasn't so bad. There was a trick Val had learned when her mother was dying of forgetting about everything except schoolwork, and concentrating completely on that. So she focused her mind on French irregular verbs and the molecular structure of water. If the teachers knew what was going on, if they knew more about Val's life than Val did, they gave no indication. She was called on the appropriate number of times, ignored the rest. Which was fine with her.

She had dreaded study hall, but that turned out fairly well too. Val and Michelle had study hall at the same time, and the one person she knew she couldn't deal with just then was her cousin. Her legal cousin. So she went to the library instead. Michelle never went to the library, and it was bound to be safe. Sister Rosemary, who ran the library, was strict about undue noise levels, so none of the other girls came over to her. She used the time to catch up with her math homework, which had gone undone the night before. Val smiled. She'd become undone herself the night before. The homework was merely symbolic.

Val was glad she had worked on it though when she went to math class the next period and faced her second surprise test of the week. She knew the reasons for the first one, and wondered if this test also had ulterior motives behind it, but Miss Gloski, their math teacher, had a history of not knowing what was going on outside her math room, so the odds were it was just a coincidence. Val didn't care. She liked having the math test, when the material was so fresh in her mind. The other girls groaned, but Val merely concentrated her thoughts on what she'd worked on a few minutes earlier and, to her own amusement, aced the quiz.

The bell rang for lunch, and all the self-assurance that Val had achieved in the morning vanished with the sound. I can do this, she told herself, and went to her locker to exchange her morning texts for the afternoon ones. Michelle was at her locker as well. The girls stared at each other for a moment.

"Are you okay?" Michelle asked.

"I'm fine," Val said. "Any reason why I shouldn't be?"

"I . . . it's just . . . well, I didn't think anybody else overheard us," Michelle said. "Yesterday I mean."

Val laughed. "You practically shouted it over the P.A. system," she said. "Did you honestly think no one would overhear?"

"I didn't think," Michelle said. "I'm sorry, Val. I'm really sorry."

"It's too late now," Val said. She slammed her locker shut, spun the combination lock around, then walked away to the school lunchroom. While there were no assigned seats, the girls always knew who sat with who. Val traditionally had lunch with Kit and Michelle. But that day, Michelle chose to sit with Theresa Martini, leaving the seat next to Val's empty.

"How did you do on the quiz?" Kit asked Val, as they began eating their turkey lunches.

"Fine," Val said. "I did my math homework in study hall right before."

"I wish I had study halls," Kit said. "Instead of two languages."

Val nodded. Kit was smarter than she was, and Jamey pushed her harder. Val didn't think her father really cared what kind of grades she got, as long as they were passing, and she didn't cause any trouble at school. Jamey expected six academic subjects and A's in all of them from Kit. On the other hand, Val suspected, he wouldn't care if any of the teachers complained that Kit showed a lack of respect.

The seat next to Val's didn't stay empty. Val could see a few of the girls talking, and one of them seemed to push Caroline O'Mara toward her. Whatever Caroline's motivation, she sat down next to Val.

"Hi," Caroline said. "Uh, how did you do on the quiz?"

"Fine," Val said. She would have preferred anyone, even Michelle, to Caroline at that moment. She waited for Kit to rescue her, but Kit seemed nonplussed.

"I hate surprise quizzes," Caroline said. "I hate turkey too. At least the way they make it here. It's always so dry."

"Is it?" Kit asked, taking an extra-large bite. "I think it's delicious."

Val didn't know what to think, since her taste buds had deserted her along with her sanity.

"Uh, some of the girls thought I ought to talk with you," Caroline said. "I don't want to bother you or anything, but, well, if you want to talk, I'd be happy to."

"Talk about what?" Val asked, and knew immediately that that was a mistake.

"About the math quiz maybe?" Kit asked. "That second problem was a killer."

"They were all killers," Caroline said. "At least to me. I never do well on surprise tests. I flunked the one in English yesterday too, I'm sure. I don't like anything to do with surprises. My mother says if she ever gave me a surprise birthday party, I'd run away from home. That's kind of a joke in our family. I wouldn't really run away. Just that I hate surprises so much."

Val took a bite of turkey and looked casually at Caroline. She had never been to any of Caroline's birthday parties, surprise or otherwise. There was no school rule saying all girls must be invited to all parties, and from kindergarten on, Val had realized some girls simply never invited her to their houses. Caroline was one of them, which was why this sudden burst of solicitude was even more appalling.

It had bothered Kit far more, Val realized, not to be invited into all those homes, but then Kit didn't have Val's large, close-knit family as a substitute. Neither did Val, not anymore. She nearly choked on some mashed potato.

"I don't know if you know it," Caroline said. "But I'm adopted."

Val nodded. She was having a hard enough time swallowing without having to comment on Caroline's private history.

Kit pushed her empty plate away. She was the fastest eater Val knew, except maybe for Jamey. "I have a cousin who's adopted," she said. "Maybe the two of you know each other."

Caroline ignored her. "Everybody's talking," she said, and Val could see that Caroline really wasn't being bitchy, that she really was concerned. "About what Michelle said yesterday. I know I'm butting in, but I thought I should talk with you. In case it's true, what Michelle said."

"Michelle said a lot of things," Kit declared. "Most of them about my mother."

Val knew what it cost Kit to bring her mother up, but it was a gift she didn't want. "It's all right," she said to her friend. "Let Caroline talk."

"Is it true?" Caroline asked. "I'm not asking to be nosy. It's just I don't want to give you a speech, to tell you personal stuff about me, if I don't have to." She smiled at Val, and for the first time Val regretted never having been welcome at the O'Mara house.

"I don't know for sure," Val said. "My father's in Washington, so I haven't spoken to him. But it might be. I mean, I won't really know until I talk to my father, but . . . Kit thinks it's true, don't you, Kit?"

Kit looked annoyed. "This isn't about me," she said.

Caroline glanced over at Kit. "You've finished your lunch already?" she said. "I get an upset stomach if I eat too fast."

"I do everything fast," Kit said.

Caroline nodded. "Since you've finished eating, do you think maybe you could leave Val and me alone?" she asked. "What we're going to talk about is private."

"Val?" Kit asked.

Val nodded.

"All right," Kit said. "I'll be in the library if you need me." She got her school books and left.

Caroline laughed. "Kit's such a strange person," she said. "I think you're the only real friend she has."

"Kit has friends," Val said.

Caroline shook her head. "Not really," she replied. "A lot of the girls like her, because she's smart and funny and she isn't mean. But no one's really close to her except you."

"Do you like her?" Val asked. It seemed a safe question, and she took a final bite of turkey after asking it.

"I don't know," Caroline said. "I don't know her very well. My father doesn't approve. . . . Well, you know how it is."

Val knew only too well. "There are people who don't think we're as good as they are," her father had told her, when she hadn't been invited to Sheila Kennedy's sixth birthday party. "They're stupid people, bigots, but we're stuck on the same planet with them. And I'm paying lots of money to send you to a school with them so you can know all different kinds of girls, from good families, even if those good families don't let you into their houses."

Val had a vague memory that she was crying. She could still picture her father picking her up and hugging her. "We're as good as anybody," he had said. "Don't you ever forget that. I'm a respectable businessman, same as all those other fathers. I went to college too, same as them. You go to school, obey the sisters, and they'll see you're a nice girl, and they'll start forgetting who your daddy is, and start asking you to be their friend."

Only it hadn't worked that way. Val merely stopped caring that she wasn't invited to half her classmates' parties. It bothered Kit far longer. Val remembered laughing at Kit when she was upset as late as sixth grade over an unextended invitation. To Caroline O'Mara's, if she remembered correctly.

"I'm sorry," Caroline said. "I know I'm not handling this well. I wish we were closer. It would be easier then."

"It's all right," Val said. "It's not your fault your parents are . . ." she almost said "bigots" but managed to stop herself in time.

"Conservative," Caroline said with a smile.

Val nodded. "Conservative," she said.

"I really love them," Caroline declared. "I always have. I was adopted as a newborn. I don't remember any other family."

"Do you wonder about them?" Val asked.

"Now and then," Caroline said. "A lot when I was about twelve. You know how it is. You'd get so mad at your mother when she wouldn't let you have something you wanted, or she'd embarrass you in public."

Val nodded, but she had only the haziest idea of what Caroline was talking about. Her mother was ill when Val was twelve, and she couldn't remember ever allowing herself to be angry or embarrassed.

"I'd think about my mother a lot then," Caroline said. "My natural mother, I mean. How perfect she must be. How much she must miss me. Once I even told my mother she wasn't my real mother, just to make her cry."

"Did you?" Val asked. "Make her cry, I mean."

Caroline shook her head. "She just shouted back," she said. "Told me I was mean and ungrateful. Which I was. So I ran to my room and slammed my door, which I did all the time back then, and I thought about what my life would have been like if they hadn't adopted me. At first it seemed all wonderful, like my natural parents would have loved me so much more and let me have whatever I wanted. But then I had to figure out why they'd given me up in the first place if they loved me that much."

Val inhaled sharply. She'd forgotten in all this that she had other parents, at least another mother, maybe another father as well, and they too had given her away. It was too much to deal with. She tried to concentrate on Caroline instead.

Caroline stared down at her plate. "I've always known I was adopted," she said. "My parents never lied to me about it. I had all the books too, all the picture books and story books and nonfiction books about being adopted. And my parents really love me. So do my grandparents. They never treated me any differently from their other grandchildren. Believe me, when I was twelve, I was looking for slights, and there just weren't any."

"What are you saying?" Val asked. "That it's okay to be adopted?"

"I'm not sure what I'm saying," Caroline replied. "I guess I feel bad for you because of how you learned it. I'm glad I've always known. My parents brought me up to feel special just because I am adopted. I'm glad my mother screamed at me that day, instead of crying. I knew then she really was my mother, because mothers get mad at their kids, and they scream, and they don't always let them have what they want. I don't know how I'd feel if someone just told me out of the blue that I was adopted. I think it would terrify me."

"I'm not terrified," Val said. "I don't even know for sure that it is true."

"I think it must be," Caroline said. "From the way Michelle's behaving. You can tell she knows she did something terrible, but she's so defensive about it. She won't say it's a lie though. I think if it was, she'd be admitting it to everybody."

"True or not, she shouldn't have said it," Val declared. "At least not here, not in public. It's a family matter, and it should be kept private."

"I guess that's why she feels so bad," Caroline said. "Not just telling you, but telling you in public."

Caroline's father was a banker. Her mother played golf. Val had driven past their house often enough to know they had beautiful flowerbeds in front. They had less land than the Castaladis, but their yard seemed larger, because they had no gate around it.

"How were you adopted?" Val asked. "Do you know?"

"From an agency," Caroline said. "My parents showed me all the paperwork. I don't know anything about my mother, my natural mother I mean, except her family medical history, which looked pretty boring to me. I guess I'll care more about that when I have babies."

"Do you want to know?" Val asked.

"Sometimes," Caroline said. "But not as much as you might think. I haven't even thought about her in a year or so. Things have been going so well in my life. My mother turned out to be okay, once I stopped being twelve. I'm glad I was adopted through an agency though. I like the fact that it was a traditional adoption, nothing gray market about it."

"Gray market," Val said. "What's that?"

"You know," Caroline said. "Not done through an agency. Lawyers handle it instead, or doctors. Or a couple puts an ad in the paper and hopes some pregnant woman will see it and contact them. Lots of adoptions are done that way nowadays. But you know my father, old straight-and-narrow. My parents waited five years before the agency came through with me. Five years. But they didn't have to worry that maybe it wasn't completely legal or the mother might change her mind the minute she gave birth. And I like the fact my natural mother went through an agency too. It makes me feel respectable, like my parents."

"Five years is a long time to wait," Val said. "I guess your mother must have known about it. The adoption I mean."

Caroline gave her a funny look. "Of course she did. Mothers always know. You think fathers just bring babies home and hand them over? It never works that way."

Val nodded. "I guess I wasn't thinking," she said. "This whole business has been real upsetting. Just being this angry at Michelle is upsetting. And I've never really thought about adoption before."

Caroline looked away from Val, then turned back to face her. "You might as well know what they're saying," she declared. "You'll hear it anyway, and I don't think Kit will tell you."

"What?" Val asked. "What are they saying?" What could be left to say?

"I'm sure it isn't true," Caroline said. "Michelle certainly hasn't said it. It's just a rumor. You know how rumors are. Maybe I shouldn't even tell you."

"You began already, so finish," Val said.

Caroline nodded. "They're saying, well, because of who your father is, they're saying maybe you weren't adopted," she replied. "Not the way I was, I mean. They're saying maybe your parents were so desperate for a baby, they did something illegal to get one."

"Illegal?" Val asked.

"Kidnapping," Caroline said. "Maybe they kidnapped a baby. Or even killed someone to get one. I'm sure they're wrong. I mean, how could they know, unless Michelle said something, and she didn't. Or maybe Kit, and she certainly didn't. It's just gossip because of your father's reputation."

"What reputation?" Val asked, even though she knew the answer.

"That he's connected," Caroline said. "With the mob. Well, you know."

Val nodded. In a life filled with things she wasn't supposed to know, that was the one thing she did.

Caroline got up. "I'm sorry," she said. "I've probably handled all this really badly. The other girls, they just thought we should talk, because I'm adopted, and now I guess you are too. And I'm sure when you talk to your father, you'll find out everything is okay. That you were adopted from an agency, the same as me, I mean. I don't think you were kidnapped. I probably never should have even mentioned it."

"No," Val said. "You probably shouldn't have."

Caroline gave Val a look so strange it took her a moment to realize it was fear. "Forget I said anything, all right," she whispered. "I didn't mean it."

Val nodded. She watched as Caroline ran back to her safe circle of friends, the girls who never invited Val to their parties. Then she looked down at the half-eaten remains of her lunch, and willed herself to ignore the horror that was growing like a tumor inside her.

Chapter 5

• • •

KIT KEPT HER distance from Val the rest of the school day, but Val didn't mind. When the final bell rang, Val walked over to her and said, "I want to go to your house."

"That's not such a good idea," Kit replied, looking down at her desk.

Val was aware that everyone in the classroom, including Sister Gina Marie, was staring at her. "Please," she whispered. "I can't go home."

Kit looked up. "All right," she said. She followed Val out of the room and to their lockers. Val noticed Michelle standing by hers, looking ill at ease. She wished worse than that for Michelle. She wished her half the pain she was currently feeling.

She and Kit walked out of the school silently, and found Bruno waiting for them. "I'm going to Kit's," Val told him.

"Fine," Bruno said. "Hop in, girls."

So they did. Kit stared out the window. Val asked Bruno how his day had been.

"Average," Bruno replied, which was the best Val could hope for. An average day meant he hadn't spent it worrying about her. And that meant another day before she would have to confront her father. Or was he her kidnapper?

Bruno dropped them off in front of the Farrell house. He never drove off until he was sure Val was safely inside. This time was no exception.

"There's a guy out there," he said, pointing toward Kit's front door. "Want me to check him out?"

"It's all right," Kit said. "Just my cousin. Thanks anyway, Bruno."

"I'll wait around," Bruno said. "Just to be on the safe side."

Val got out of the car. She felt past the point of needing protection. "Your cousin?" she asked Kit.

"My cousin," Kit replied. "I invited him over this morning. I didn't know you'd be coming over."

Val felt hurt, even though she knew it was irrational. Somehow she felt Kit should have known she would need her. "Why did you ask him?" she said. "I didn't know you were that close to any of your cousins."

"Hi, Malcolm!" Kit shouted at him. Val could see he was young, maybe a year or two older than they were. He had a preppy look to him. She remembered Kit referring to a cousin who was going to college nearby. The Farrells had had him over for dinner a couple of times.

"Hi, Kit!" he called back. That seemed to satisfy Bruno, who finally drove off. Val almost cried for him to come back and get her. She felt that Kit was cutting her off too, that the last part of her life that was secure and reliable was being lost to her.

"You're early," Kit said to her cousin as she reached the front door. She took out her keys and unlocked it.

"My class was cancelled," Malcolm replied. "So I figured I'd come straight over. I've only been waiting a couple of minutes."

"This is Val," Kit said. "Val Castaladi. Val, this is my cousin, Malcolm Scott."

"It's nice to meet you," Val said.

"Good meeting you," Malcolm said. He smiled, and Val could see he was good-looking. Light brown hair, blue eyes. He didn't look anything like a Farrell, so he must come from Amanda's side of the family.

"I did a lot of work on the house last night, but I couldn't fix everything," Kit said. "The kitchen's in okay shape, but, the more I looked, the more I saw Mother had done. And Pop didn't get in until really late last night. So the living room still has some problems. But we can sit down in it and everything. It's just I had to take down some of the paintings, so they're on the floor." She smiled apologetically.

"It looks fine to me," Malcolm said. "I guess Jamey'll use it as an excuse to buy some new paintings."

"I don't know," Kit said. "I don't think so. I don't think the insurance is going to cover the damage, since Mother did it, and the clinic she's at is real expensive."

"Oh," Malcolm said. "Sorry."

"It's not the end of the world," Kit replied. "Would either of you like something to drink?"

"Ginger ale, if you have it," Malcolm said. He sat down on the sofa, beside a blank wall. Val remembered the painting that had hung there. It wasn't the one she'd seen slashed the day before. Amanda must really have gone mad on Sunday.

"Me too," she said.

"Okay," Kit said. She walked to the kitchen, then came back almost instantly. "I forgot," she said. "Pop got home so late yesterday we didn't buy any groceries. There's a can of frozen lemonade, if you want me to make that instead."

"Sounds good," Malcolm said.

"I don't know how Mother missed it," Kit called from the kitchen. "She went through the freezer. She found an ice cream carton and threw it into the broom closet. That was a mess to clean up, let me tell you."

"I wish you'd called me," Malcolm said. "I would have gathered up some guys from my dorm, and we could have had a scrubbing party."

Kit brought in the pitcher of lemonade and three unmatched glasses. "Next time," she said.

Val stared at them. She'd never seen Kit talk to anyone that way, except herself. Kit couldn't keep her mother's problems a secret, Amanda saw to that, but she didn't go around advertising them.

"It's okay," Kit said to Val. "Malcolm's a trusty."

Val smiled. She hadn't heard Kit use that term in years. A trusty was one of the rare people Kit found trustworthy. Val was one, and her mother had been until her death. Jamey was another, and Sister Angela, their third-grade teacher. It was a short list. Malcolm should be honored to be on it.

"I take that as a compliment," he said, picking up one of the lemonade glasses and drinking from it.

"It is," Val said. "Maybe Kit'll even let you scrub next time."

"Have you heard anything from your mother?" Malcolm asked.

Kit shook her head. "Pop called the clinic yesterday, to make sure she was okay, but she isn't allowed to talk to anybody for the first few days. I'm not sure if that's for her sake or ours."

"How's Jamey dealing with it?" Malcolm asked.

"I'm not sure," Kit replied. "He's avoiding it, he's avoiding me. I'm sorry, Malcolm. I really didn't ask you over to unload all this on you."

"I can deal with it," he said. "I come from the stable side of the family, remember." He turned, and smiled at Val. "Do you have one of those?" he asked. "A stable family?"

"Val's the one I told you about," Kit said.

"You told him about me?" Val asked. "What exactly did you tell him?"

"Calm down," Malcolm said. "Kit just told me you'd found out recently that you were adopted. That's all. I'm adopted, so she wanted to talk with me. Get a few pointers in the adoption game, that's all."

"Wasn't Caroline enough for one day?" Val cried. "Do I have to talk to him too?"

"I didn't invite Caroline to our table," Kit said. "And if you remember correctly, I didn't invite you here either. I told you it wasn't a good idea, but you insisted on coming over anyway. Remember?"

Val nodded. "I'm sorry," she said. "If you want, I'll go."

"Only if you want," Kit said. "Malcolm, I hope you don't mind. Val only found out yesterday, I'm not even sure of all the details, and she had a rough time at school today."

"I'll bet," Malcolm said. "Have you spoken to your parents about it? Is that how you found out?"

"My mother's dead," Val replied. "My father's out of town on business. My cousin Michelle told me yesterday at school. She was angry, and it just came out."

"Then you can't be sure it is true," Malcolm declared. "Maybe she lied."

"She didn't," Val said. "I found a letter my mother wrote me. She wanted me to read it on my eighteenth birthday. It's all about how she wanted a baby and couldn't have one, so my father brought me to her."

"What?" Malcolm said. "That isn't how people adopt."

"That isn't how Caroline O'Mara got adopted, that's for sure," Val said. "Her parents waited five years before the agency found them a baby. No shortcuts for them."

"There's nothing wrong with shortcuts," Malcolm said. "I'm gray market myself, although my parents wouldn't appreciate the term. They wanted a baby, and my mom's doctor knew about a girl who was pregnant and didn't feel she could raise her child by herself, so my parents offered to adopt. And that's why I'm Malcolm Scott and not Joe Bloke."

"Maybe that's what your mother meant," Kit said. "In her letter."

Val shook her head. "Mama didn't know anything about me," she said. "She called me a gift. Like I was something my father went to a store and bought."

"I don't know anything about your father," Malcolm said. "But that's just not how adoptions work. At least not legal adoptions."

"So how can you be sure it was legal?" Val asked. "Maybe it wasn't."

"Jamey's your father's lawyer, right?" Malcolm said. "He wouldn't let one of his clients do anything like that, would he, Kit."

"What exactly did Caroline say to you?" Kit asked.

"You must know," Val said. "You must have heard it too. Where I came from was the hot topic in school today."

"I don't understand any of this," Malcolm said. "I can see where people would be interested to find out someone's adopted, especially if they didn't know. I never told a lot of people, and when anyone found out, I had to go through the inquisition all over again. But nobody speculated about where I came from. Not even me. At least not in public."

Val stared at her glass of lemonade. "I hate lemonade," she said. "Why did you bring me any?"

"Sorry," Kit said. "I forgot." She moved the glass away from Val.

"Castaladi," Malcolm said. "Isn't there a crime family named Castaladi?"

"My father's a businessman," Val said. "He owns a construction business."

Malcolm turned to Kit. "What kind of law does your father do, anyway?"

"He won't end up on the Supreme Court, if that's what you're asking," Kit replied.

Malcolm grinned. "When I came out east to college, my parents warned me about the sorts of people I'd meet," he said. "But I've got to say, the two of you look pretty harmless."

"My father is not a criminal," Val said. "All my life I've had to put up with whispers. Kit knows what it's been like. Half the girls at Most Precious Blood won't have anything to do with me. Her either, for that matter, just because her father's my father's lawyer."

"That stinks," Malcolm said. "Why'd your parents put up with that?"

Val fell silent.

"I don't think Val's mother understood what it was like," Kit replied slowly. "She was really kind of sheltered, mostly did things with her family. And Val's father took those kinds of slights for granted. I think he assumed it was part of getting a good education."

"And your parents?" Malcolm asked.

"It drove my mother crazy," Kit said. "Among other things. And Pop just figures if Kevin and I are the best, the world will come to us in due course."

"I'm sorry," Malcolm said. "There was one kid I knew who used to really go at me because I was adopted. Claimed that meant for sure I was illegitimate, which I assume I am, but what's the big deal. He called me a bastard once too often, and I broke his nose."

"Really?" Kit asked.

Malcolm grinned. "The only time in my life I ever got into a fight," he said. "Lucky punch. My parents were hysterical. I wasn't allowed TV for two weeks, but it was worth it. At least he stopped calling me a bastard where I could hear him."

"That's what Michelle said I was," Val said. "My father's bastard, who he just brought home for my mother to raise."

"I don't think so," Kit said. "Rick always seemed to love your mother. I can't see him cheating on her like that, let alone making her raise his kid without even telling her."

"Maybe your father hired a surrogate to have a child," Malcolm suggested. "She could have been impregnated by artificial insemination. It's a little strange that he didn't tell your mother, but it was probably legal. Jamey might well have handled the paperwork."

Val thought about it. "Do you realize that's the best possible explanation?" she said. "That's how pathetic things are right now, that I'm relieved at the thought he hired a surrogate without telling Mama."

"Are there other alternatives?" Malcolm asked. "Besides your cousin Michelle's version."

"Plenty," Val said. "At least according to Caroline." She felt better knowing there was another explanation, one without violence or betrayal. "The girls at school think maybe I was kidnapped. Snatched so my parents could have a child to raise. Or maybe they had my parents killed." She felt tears welling in her eyes. "I'm sorry," she said. "It's just I always knew who my parents were, and now I don't know anything anymore."

Kit ran to the kitchen and brought back an unopened box of tissues. Val tore it open, and pulled a tissue out. It felt strange to cry in front of Malcolm, but she knew it was okay. He was a trusty. Kit said so.

"Do your parents love you?" Malcolm asked her.

Val nodded.

"Then it can't be too bad," Malcolm said. "Whatever the explanation is, I'm sure it's all perfectly legal."

"Do you think so?" Val asked Kit. "You know my father. Do you think he could have just stolen me?"

"I can't answer that," Kit said. "I don't have as high an opinion of parents as the two of you do. They're just adults with children, and adults do strange things."

"You're wrong," Val said. "Not about your parents maybe, but about mine. Daddy's a businessman. He's not responsible for what his father used to do, what his brother might do. He builds buildings. He's built half the condos in this town. He doesn't kill people or kidnap them, and I won't have anyone saying otherwise."

"Good," Malcolm said. "That's settled. Now maybe we should talk about other things."

But before they had a chance to find something safe to talk about, the doorbell rang. Kit got up and answered it.

"I need to talk to Val. Connie told me she was here."

It was Terry. "I'm in here," Val called from the living room. Terry followed Kit in.

"I've never been in here before," Terry said. "It's a nice house, Kit."

"Thank you," Kit said. "Terry, this is my cousin Malcolm. Malcolm, this is Terry Bellini. She's Val's father's cousin's wife.

"Pleased to meet you," Malcolm said, getting up. Terry nodded at him.

"We need to talk, Val," Terry said.

"We can talk here," Val replied. "Malcolm and Kit know what's going on."

"Michelle went a little crazy yesterday," Terry said. "Because of Sunday. She was upset about Sunday."

Val examined Terry closely. She could see the remnants of a bruised eye under the heavy makeup. "I'm sorry," she said. "I should have come over the way you wanted."

"That's water under the bridge," Terry replied. "What's important now is you."

Terry had been her mother's matron of honor, Val thought. Terry was one of who knew how many people in on her parents' secret. Hell, Michelle had learned it from Terry and Bob. All the Castaladis knew, and so did her mother's whole family. For sixteen years, they'd managed to keep it a secret from her.

"I'm all right," Val said.

"Michelle had no right to tell you," Terry said. "I don't know how she knew. She must have overheard something once. I swear I never told her. I'm going to punish her, I just don't know how yet. It has to be some way Bob doesn't figure out. If he should hear, he'd go crazy."

Val pictured Bob attacking Michelle. He would do it

too, she knew, if he thought Michelle had caused a permanent rift between him and her father. Rather than think about it, she took a sip of the lemonade.

"I love you like a daughter, Val," Terry said. "When your mother was dying, I promised her I'd look after you, see to it that you always had a family, had people you could turn to. And we've never once had a family occasion without asking you and Ricky first. You sit at our table. We share the same blood."

"I don't," Val said. The words sounded harsh, artificial, but she had to say them, if for no other reason than to see Terry's reaction.

Terry looked stricken. "Your parents love you," she said. "Your mother would have cut out her heart for you. You couldn't be more precious to your father if you were his own."

"What do you want, Terry?" Kit asked.

"Have you told him?" Terry asked. "Does Rick know yet what Michelle did?"

"Not yet," Val replied. "He's still in Washington."

Terry's relief was visible. "Thank God," she said. "Promise me you won't tell him."

"Wait a second," Malcolm said. "I don't mean to butt in here, but isn't that between Val and her father?"

"You can't tell him you found out from Michelle," Terry said. "You want to talk to Ricky about it, I can't stop you. Maybe you have a right to know. But I don't know what he'll do if he finds out Michelle's responsible. Val, listen to me. Ricky could destroy us. He'll know Michelle heard it from Bob and me. If he thinks we've hurt you in any way . . ." She began to sob.

Malcolm looked stunned. Kit tossed the box of tissues over to Terry.

"I can't make any promises," Val said. "Not until I know just how I was adopted. Tell me the truth, Terry, and I won't have to talk to my father."

"I don't know the truth," Terry said. "None of us do. Your parents wanted a baby, your mother was sick with grief she didn't have one. One day, your father brings one home. He never offers any explanation where the baby came from, not to your mother or to Bob, or to anybody I know. He must have told his father. But I don't think anybody else knows. He's head of the house. It's no one else's business."

"That's crazy," Malcolm said. "Adoptions simply don't work that way."

Terry ignored him. "Your father's a hard man," she said to Val. "I know to you he's your daddy, he loves you and gives you things. You go sailing together. But he takes what he wants, and he doesn't care who he hurts. And if someone hurts him, he destroys them. I don't know how he got you, and I don't want to know. If you know what's good for you, you won't want to know either. And if he should find out Michelle's involved, he'll hurt her somehow, an accident to her or me or Bob. I'm begging you, Val. Don't tell him how you found out. You'll keep the whole business to yourself if you're smart. But if you can't do that, at least don't tell him Michelle's to blame. What happens to her, to us, will be on your head."

"I think that's enough," Kit said. "You made your speech, Terry. Val's heard you."

"It's all right," Val said. "I promise I'll leave all of you out of it."

Terry ran over to her and kissed her. Val's face grew wet from Terry's tears. "You're a good girl, Val," she said. "Your mama loved you from the moment she saw you."

Val nodded. She watched as Terry blew her nose, then said goodbye to all of them, and left the room. Kit followed her out.

"I'm sorry," Val said to Malcolm. "I don't know what you must think."

"I don't know what I think either," he said. "Except that if I were you, I'd go see Jamey and make sure everything is on the up and up before I saw your father."

Val nodded. "I'll go now," she said. "While I'm still too scared not to."

Chapter 6

• • •

"**A**RE YOU SURE Jamey doesn't know what's going on?" Val asked as she put her jacket on.

Kit sighed. "For the hundredth time, he doesn't know," she replied. "He got in after midnight last night. When he saw my light on, he peeked in and apologized for leaving me with the mess. That was the extent of our conversation. He was still sleeping when I left for school this morning. He doesn't suspect a thing."

"All right," Val said. "I just have the feeling I'll get a straighter answer from him if I catch him unawares."

"He'll be shocked," Kit said. "I guarantee it."

"I'm not wild about leaving you alone," Malcolm said to Kit. "We haven't really talked."

"Some other time," Kit said. "Give Val a lift to Pop's, then go back to school. I still have a ton of homework to catch up with, and then I have to make supper."

"You sure?" Malcolm asked.

"Positive," Kit replied. "Now get out, both of you."

Val and Malcolm left the house. Malcolm kept looking back as they walked toward his car.

"Kit's okay," Val told him as he unlocked the doors. "She deals better with things alone."

"She has a lot to deal with," Malcolm said.

"She's used to it," Val replied. "This isn't the first Amanda crisis. I doubt it'll be the last."

Malcolm pulled out of his parking space and began the short drive to Jamey's office. "The two of you have been friends for long?" he asked.

"Since birth," Val replied, but then she laughed. "Since shortly after birth. Nothing's since birth anymore."

"You must really be shaken up," he said.

Val nodded. "I'm so confused I don't know what I feel anymore," she said. "I love my father. I can't believe all those things people have been saying, but I can't believe him either. Not the way I used to. I keep thinking this is all a bad dream, that I'll wake up and it'll be Monday morning, and none of this will have happened."

"I had a dog that died a couple of years ago," Malcolm said. "An Irish setter. We'd had him for seven years. I took him out for a walk, and I don't know, something made him run into the street and a car hit him. It was a week before I really believed he was dead. I kept thinking it was a bad dream, even though I saw it happen."

Val was silent.

"It isn't much," Malcolm said. "But life's really pretty normal in Indiana. Christmas trees and picket fences and renting a tux for the senior prom. Things are definitely different in the east."

Val laughed. "I think you picked an unusual couple of days here," she said.

"I should hope so," Malcolm replied. "I'd hate to think every day is like this."

"Make the next left," Val said. "Jamey's office is four blocks down."

Malcolm followed Val's directions. "Do you know what you're going to say to him?" he asked.

"I'll know when I see him," Val replied, hoping that was true.

"Do you want me to come in with you?"

"No," Val said. "Go back to school. I don't know how long it'll take."

"How will you get home?" he asked.

"I'll call for a cab," Val replied. "I'm not helpless. I know it must seem that way right now, but I'm perfectly capable of getting from one place to another." She paused for a moment and realized ordinarily she'd call Bruno and wait for him to take her. She wondered if ordinarily would ever return to her life.

Malcolm dropped her off in front of Jamey's office building. Val grabbed her books, thanked him, and watched as he drove off. Bruno wouldn't have just left her there, she thought. Was this what life outside the Castaladi circle was like?

She entered the building, got onto the elevator, and took it to the third floor. Jamey had had the same office for years now. She could remember playing there with Kit and even Kevin when they were all little kids.

Jamey had a new secretary, prettier than the last one, Val noticed. "I'm Val Castaladi," she said, and the name sounded strange to her, untrue. "I'd like to see Jamey if he's free."

"I'll check," the secretary said. She buzzed Jamey's office and told him Val was there.

"Send her in," Jamey said over the intercom. Val smiled at the secretary and went in. She always liked Jamey's office, the way the walls were lined with law books, the family pictures on the desk, the window overlooking the main street in town. Jamey's office looked homey, in a way his home never had.

"Val," Jamey said, getting up and giving her a hug. "This is a pleasant surprise. Sit down. Tell me what brings you to my section of town."

Val smiled at him. Jamey looked exactly like Kit, small and wiry with reddish-blond hair and green eyes. They had the same smiles too, smiles that lit up a room. Val tried to remember the last time she'd seen Kit smile that way, without irony or rue.

"Actually, I'm glad you came," Jamey said. "Although I wouldn't have called you. How's Kit doing?"

"How do you mean?" Val asked.

"This business with Amanda shook us hard," Jamey replied. "Have you been over to the house?"

"I was there yesterday," Val said. "I helped a little with the cleaning."

Jamey frowned. "Kit won't tell me the complete story," he declared. "She was alone with Amanda for close to half an hour, before I could get there. I tried to get her to talk to me when we drove back from the clinic Sunday night, but you know Kit. She just kept it to herself. I thought maybe she was talking to you."

"The place was a mess," Val said. "I know that."

"I'm not a very good father," Jamey said. "That isn't something I admit very often even to myself. I'm a worse husband, if that's any comfort. I don't know how to deal with people I love. Kevin's easy. He handles things through avoidance. That's a pattern I can understand. He doesn't want to come home, fine. I'm more than happy to pay for prep schools and colleges and summers abroad. But Kit insists on staying, taking care of things. She meets everything head on."

"Isn't that good?" Val asked. "Isn't that how you're supposed to handle things?"

"Not when you're still a kid," Jamey said. "Not when you can't possibly handle the things you're confronting. How is Kit supposed to deal with Amanda's drinking? I can't, and I'm a good thirty years older than Kit is."

"I don't know," Val said.

"Neither do I," Jamey said. "But I'm open to suggestions."

Val thought about how Jamey had been away on Sunday, stayed away on Monday. She thought about Kit all alone in the house with the torn paintings and the slashed mattress. She wondered, not for the first time, about just how closely Jamey adhered to his marriage vows, and whether Kit was as suspicious of those pretty secretaries Jamey favored as she was.

"Maybe you could spend more time with her," she said. "The two of you could do something together, the way . . ." She wanted to say, "the way Daddy and I do," but the words wouldn't come out.

"The way families are supposed to," Jamey said. "It's an interesting concept. Kit and I do approximate the average American family a lot more when Amanda's drying out, I know that. I guess we could do something together. What do you and Rick do? Sail? Anything else?"

"He takes me out to dinner sometimes," Val said. "And we watch movies together on the VCR. It doesn't have to be anything fancy."

"Maybe the four of us could get together," Jamey said. "Over the weekend maybe. Sunday brunch. How does that sound?"

Val had no idea how it sounded, but she suspected Kit would like it a lot. "Why don't you and Kit count on doing it," she said. "And if Daddy and I can join you, we will."

Jamey nodded. "Fair enough," he said. "Thank you. Is that why you dropped in, to talk to me about Kit?"

"Frankly, no," Val said. "It's more like a legal matter."

Jamey raised his eyebrows. "How legal?" he asked. "Trouble at school?"

"Nothing like that," Val said. She bit down on her lower lip and willed the words to come out.

"Drugs?" Jamey asked. "Alcohol? Are you pregnant?"

Val raised her hand to stop him. "No," she said. "I'm not in trouble. I just need some information."

"For a paper?" Jamey asked. "Social studies maybe?"

"Jamey, please," Val said. "This is hard for me, and you're not making it any easier."

"Sorry," he said. "Take your time."

"It has to do with my parents," Val said. "My real parents."

"Your real parents?" Jamey said.

"I know I'm adopted," Val said.

"What makes you say that?" Jamey asked.

"I found a letter my mother wrote me," Val said. "For me to read on my eighteenth birthday. I didn't bother waiting. I read it last night. She said I was adopted, and I don't see any reason to think she'd lie."

"Have you spoken to your father about this?" Jamey asked.

"No," Val said. "He's in Washington. You know that."

"So why are you speaking to me?" Jamey asked.

"You're his lawyer," Val said. "And his friend. You must know about the adoption."

"I'm not saying that I do," Jamey replied. "But if I did, what would you expect me to tell you?"

"Everything," Val said. "My mother's letter told me practically nothing. She didn't seem to know where I came from, how Daddy got me. I've been talking to other people who are adopted, and they all tell me both parents always know. You don't just bring a baby home one day, the way Daddy seems to have. I figure if Mama didn't know, you must. I want to hear everything."

"I'm sorry," Jamey said. "I can certainly understand your feelings, but there's nothing I can do to help you, except to suggest that you talk to Rick about it."

"Come on, Jamey," Val said. "I can't, and you know it. You think I can just wait for Daddy to get home and casually ask him if he kidnapped me as an infant? Or if he had an affair with someone, and I'm his illegitimate child?"

"Where do you get these ideas?" Jamey asked.

"What am I supposed to think?" Val replied. "That Daddy found an agency that never bothered to ask what Mama felt? That he convinced some doctor somewhere to find him a baby and not ever mention it to Mama, so it could be a surprise?"

"I'm surprised by you," Jamey said. "Rick's been a wonderful father, especially since your mother died. I've never known a father and daughter who were closer than the two of you. I flounder around with Kit, can't even comfort her when Amanda goes on one of her drunken rampages, and you question your father and his love for you?"

"No," Val said. "I don't question that. At least I don't think I do. But I do question why he kept my adoption a secret from me, and whether it was legal. And I also question why you won't just tell me what I want to know."

"Because I'm his lawyer," Jamey replied. "And we have

a lawyer-client relationship that guarantees confidentiality, no matter how pressing your needs are. I can't answer any of your questions, Val. I can only suggest you ask Rick yourself."

"And what if he lies to me?" Val asked. "The way he's been lying for sixteen years?"

"Then you'll have to get your answers some other way," Jamey said.

"Can't you tell me anything?" Val cried. "Can't you tell me at least if my parents, my real parents, are alive? Nobody was murdered to get me, were they?"

"You can't honestly believe that," Jamey said. "You think Rick shot up a nursery somewhere, stashed the machine gun in the bushes, and brought you home to your mother?"

"Does that mean he didn't?" Val asked.

"The very idea is absurd," Jamey declared. "As you well know."

"Tell me this then," Val said. "Were you his lawyer then? If I am legally adopted, did you handle the paperwork?"

"I was his lawyer then," Jamey replied. "And because of that, I can't tell you anything more. Ask Rick. He'll be home soon enough."

"I don't understand you," Val said. "All my life you've told me if I ever need help, I can turn to you. And now the one time I do, you tell me to get out. If you're like this with Kit, I really feel sorry for her."

Jamey was silent for a moment. "I feel sorry for her too," he said. "Val, I've been your father's lawyer for twenty years now. I was fresh out of law school when he hired me. He's my best friend, and I'm his. I was the first person he called when his wife died. He's Kit's godfather. It's been a constant comfort to me that Kit's had you, had your family to turn to when her own is in shambles. It breaks my heart to see you this way, angry, confused, doubting Rick's love for you, doubting Rick himself. But there's not a blessed thing I can do for you except urge you to talk to him. He's the only person who can answer your questions. I know I can't."

"That's crap," Val said. She picked up her schoolbooks from the floor and stood. "Thanks anyway."

"How are you getting home?" Jamey asked. "Is Bruno waiting for you?"

"He's home," Val said. "He doesn't know anything about this. I'll take a cab."

"I'll take you," Jamey said. "Just give me a minute."

"Don't bother," Val said. She ran out of the office and down the stairs, not even waiting for the elevator. She wondered if Jamey would call Bruno, the way Kit had, but then she didn't care. She could walk home. It was only a mile or so away.

As she walked down the main street, Val tried to remember if there had ever been a time she'd walked home alone from anywhere, even Kit's. She couldn't think of one. Someone, usually Bruno or Connie, had accompanied her. She was sixteen years old, and this was the first walk she'd ever taken all by herself. She was sixteen years old, and her life was a lie, and she was completely alone. Things had to be different in Indiana.

She could see her house a half a block away. There was the fence, wrought iron and ominous, and the evergreens that lined the property, keeping the house dark and sheltered from view. When she was younger, she thought it looked like a castle, but now it just looked like a prison.

She stood for a moment staring at her home. Her mother had loved it, she knew, but she also knew how much her mother had cherished her times away from it, especially those times she stole away from everybody. If she had run off with Val on occasion, she must have run off to be alone as well. Val pictured her mother. She didn't think about her very much, she'd almost stopped thinking about her while she was dying. It was easier to think about schoolwork.

Didn't she wonder, Val thought. Didn't she ever dare ask where her daughter came from? What kind of woman would simply accept a baby and raise it as her own without wanting to know where the baby came from, how it was acquired.

"Obedience is only right," Val's father had once told Val, on the rare occasion when she had questioned one of the sisters. "A child should obey her parents and her teachers, a wife should obey her husband."

Who should a husband obey, Val had wanted to ask, but didn't dare. Kit would have, and Jamey would have had an answer, unless it was covered by confidentiality. If Val's father had asked her mother to kill, would she have obeyed him? If he asked her to accept a kidnapped baby as her own, would she have agreed? Or would she have reported it to the police, knowing the pain some mother was going through because her child had been stolen from her.

Val stood across the street from her house and stared at the evergreens. There was one thing she knew without any confirmation and that was there was pain associated with her going to live with the Castaladis. Whose pain, she might never know. But that didn't make it any less real.

She took a deep breath and crossed the street. She couldn't imagine continuing to live under the same roof as Rick Castaladi, but she didn't know where else she could go, at least not then. She went up the front walk and unlocked the door.

"Val! Where were you?"

"Daddy?" she said, unable to stop her father from embracing her.

"Were you out by yourself?" he asked. "You should know better than that."

"I went to Kit's," Val said. "Bruno took me. I decided to walk home, that's all."

"You should have called Bruno," Rick said. "He would have gotten you."

"What kind of trouble could I get into walking home five blocks?" Val asked, knowing it wasn't from Kit's and it was more than five blocks, and she was lying to her father and she didn't care.

"Plenty," Rick said. "You could get into a lot of trouble walking home from Kit's, from school, from anywhere. The world is not all sweetness and light, Val. I pay Bruno a salary for a reason."

"I'll call next time," Val said. It was easier than arguing with him. "What are you doing home anyway? I thought you weren't getting back until tomorrow."

"That headache of yours worried me," Rick replied. "So I cancelled tomorrow's appointments and grabbed the shuttle back. Business can keep until next week. How are you feeling?"

"All right," Val said.

"Is your headache gone?" Rick asked. "Connie said you felt okay this morning, but you didn't sound quite right to me when we talked. I almost told you to stay home from school."

"I feel fine, Daddy," Val said. "You didn't have to come home early."

"You're a lot more important to me than some jerk at HUD," Rick replied. "But I don't like this. Headaches, then not calling Bruno, but taking off on your own. Are you sure everything's okay?"

"No," Val said. "It isn't."

"I knew it," Rick said. "You want to tell me what's going on?"

Val stared at the man who was what, her father, her kidnapper, and tried to follow Jamey's advice. Just ask him and wait for the happy answers. But the words were choked up inside her, and she realized that she was afraid. She had never been afraid of her father before, not even when she was little and had angered him. And now he frightened her the way he had frightened Terry.

"It's Kit," she said. "I told you Amanda's in a clinic. She got drunk on Sunday and tore up the house. She broke just about everything in the kitchen, and she even ripped some of Jamey's paintings."

"She's a very sick woman," Rick said. "I guess Kit's real upset about it."

Val nodded.

"And you've been over there, helping her out," Rick said. "Headache and all."

Val looked down at the floor.

"I hope Kit appreciates what kind of a friend she has," Rick said. "The way you stand by her, the way you're always there for her. She's a lucky girl to have you."

"Yeah," Val said. "She's real lucky."

Rick gave Val another hug. She felt her body stiffen, and tried to relax before he sensed her tension. "Tell you what," he said. "How about you go to your room, get out of that uniform, and we have dinner out together? How does Chinese sound?"

"Not tonight, Daddy," Val said. "I really should go to my room and catch up on my homework. I didn't do anything yesterday because of my headache."

"You'll get another headache if you don't eat supper," Rick said.

"I have my period," she lied, knowing Rick would be uncomfortable with that. "I feel kind of crampy."

"Poor kid," he said. "Go upstairs then, and I'll have Connie make you some tea. If you feel up to it later, we can watch a movie together."

"Okay," Val said. She forced herself to give her father a quick kiss on his cheek, then turned her back to him, and walked away from him slowly, carefully, so he couldn't see how hard she was shaking.

Chapter 7

• • •

RICK WAS ALREADY in the dining room when Val went in for breakfast. He put down his newspaper and looked at her, awaiting his morning kiss. Val walked over to him and pecked him on the cheek. She'd avoided further contact with him the night before, but she knew she'd have to see him in the morning and act as though nothing had happened. She didn't have the strength for a confrontation, not just yet.

"Sleep well?" he asked. "Feeling better now?"

"Much," Val replied.

Connie came in and asked Val what she wanted for breakfast. Val hated the thought of eating in front of her father, but knew she had no choice. "Scrambled eggs and toast," she said.

"I have some nice melon," Connie said. "I bought it yesterday. How about a slice?"

"Sure," Val replied. She glanced at her father to see if he had resumed reading the paper, but he hadn't.

"I made a few phone calls last night," he said.

"Oh?" Val said.

"Figured I might as well, let people know I'm back a little early," Rick declared. "Good thing too. Jamey tells me the shopping center in Hackensack's run into some labor problems. I'll have to go over there, talk things out with the boys."

"I hope it isn't anything serious," Val said.

"It won't be," Rick replied. "Not after a little friendly conversation."

Val nodded. "Did Jamey have anything else to say?" she managed to ask.

"He was in a funny mood," Rick said. "Distracted like. I don't think he would have brought Amanda up if I hadn't. He talked a little bit about Kit, how proud he was of her and how concerned. He usually doesn't do that, talk about his kids. I brag about you all the time, but Jamey keeps that stuff to himself. He said Kevin's doing real well at Notre Dame, but that's no surprise. That boy has a real head on his shoulders. I wouldn't be surprised if he becomes a lawyer. Like father, like son."

"I think Kit wants to be a lawyer," Val said. The Farrells suddenly seemed like a nice, safe topic.

"Daughters are different," Rick said. "You want different things for them. Homes, families. They don't have to have careers like men do."

"So you don't expect me to take over your business one day?" Val asked.

Rick laughed. "I expect you to marry a smart Italian boy, and he'll take over the business," he replied. "Kevin Farrell can be his lawyer, just like Jamey's mine. And you'll give me lots of healthy grandchildren."

"What does Kit do?" Val asked.

"That's her lookout, not ours," Rick said. "She'll probably drink like her mother."

"Daddy!" Val cried. "How can you say that?"

"Sorry, honey," Rick said. "I've seen a little more of the

world than you. I shouldn't be so cynical first thing in the morning."

Connie brought in Val's breakfast. "I made the eggs just the way you like them," she said, although she always made Val's eggs just the way she liked them. Connie did everything exactly the way she was told, including keeping secrets. She and Bruno certainly knew where their security came from.

"Thanks, Connie," Val said. She took a bite of the eggs and convinced herself she'd be able to finish them.

Connie poured Rick another cup of coffee, then left. Rick sighed contentedly.

"There's no place like home," he said. "I miss it when I'm away from here."

"I missed you," Val said, because she knew he expected her to.

"Likewise," Rick said. "I also called Terry last night. Had kind of a strange talk with her too."

"What was strange about it?" Val asked. She bit into the toast as a form of protection.

"She was in a mood too," Rick said. "I said to her maybe we'd come over tonight, make up for that dinner we both missed on Sunday, and she gave me a real song and dance why we shouldn't. This kid's busy doing this, and that kid's busy doing that, and the house is a mess, and she doesn't have anything decent to feed us. It didn't make sense to me. She'd have all day to straighten up and buy something and rearrange the kids' plans. Besides, we're family. She shouldn't feel she has to make a big fuss over us."

"It was short notice, Daddy," Val said. "Maybe we could get together over the weekend."

"That's something else," Rick said. "Jamey mentioned

maybe we'd get together for brunch on Sunday. Him and Kit and you and me. What do you think?"

"That sounds nice," Val replied.

"I guess that means we go sailing on Saturday," Rick said. "The days are getting too short to go after brunch. Especially if Jamey starts talking. We'll never get out of there."

"Sailing Saturday, brunch Sunday," Val said. "It sounds like a nice weekend."

"I agree," Rick said. "And I'm glad you think so, because I'm going to have to work late today. Catch up with everything I missed being in Washington. And that trip to Hackensack's going to take a while. Can you mange without me this evening?"

Val relaxed instantly. "I'll manage," she said.

"Want to go to Kit's after school?" Rick asked. "I can tell Jamey to take you girls out to supper someplace nice."

"No, that's all right," Val said. She finished her eggs and checked the time. "I'd better get going," she declared. "I don't want to be late."

"One more thing," Rick said. "I had a little talk with Bruno last night, about your walking home from Kit's alone."

"Daddy," Val said. "It was nothing."

"Bruno should know better than to let you do that," Rick declared. "He gets paid to keep an eye out on this family, and that includes seeing to it you aren't alone."

"It's my fault," Val said. "I should have called him, and I just didn't want to. Kit walks home by herself all the time."

"Kit isn't a Castaladi," Rick said.

Neither am I, Val wanted to say. "I'm sorry," she said instead, getting up. "It seemed like such a little thing."

"It's the little things that are dangerous," Rick said.

Val shook her head. "Is Bruno going to stay by my side forever?" she asked. "Is he going to go to college with me?"

"If you go to college, you'll go to one nearby," her father declared. "Seton Hall, maybe. You think I'm going to send you off to California somewhere, you'll live in a dorm and run around with nobody looking out for you?"

Val had given college no thought whatsoever until that moment. "Yes," she said. "That's exactly what I thought."

"Then you thought wrong," Rick said. "You'll go to a good Catholic school Bruno can drive you to, and we'll find you a nice boy, and you'll get married. You and Michelle can go together, if that makes you feel better."

"What if I want to go to school in California?" Val asked. "What if I don't want to get married? What if Michelle doesn't want to go to school with me?"

"Don't worry about Michelle," Rick said. "She'll want what we tell her to want."

"Fine," Val said. "But that doesn't help with my problems."

"You'll want what I tell you to want too," Rick said. "I don't know what's going on with you, honey, but I hope you shake this mood off soon. You've always been such a good girl, just like your mama that way, and now you're talking back to me and doing things you know you shouldn't. You got me worried."

"It's nothing, Daddy," Val said. She was shaking with anger and fear. "I'd better go."

"Bruno's in the kitchen, waiting for you," Rick said. "Have a nice day at school. I should be home before ten."

"All right," Val said. She walked over to her father, and kissed him, because not to would have caused another scene. She went to the hall closet, got her jacket and her books, then walked to the kitchen. Bruno and Connie were finishing their breakfasts, but when Bruno saw Val, he pushed his mug of coffee aside, got up and opened the garage door for her.

Val followed him to the car, climbed into the back seat, and stared out the window as Bruno drove to school. She waited for him to give her a lecture, but he kept his mouth shut. She was grateful for the silence.

Michelle was waiting for her when the car arrived. "I know Rick's back," she said. "He called Mama last night. She was hysterical all night after that."

"She shouldn't have been," Val said. "I promised her I wouldn't say anything."

"If anything happens to any of us, then it's your fault," Michelle said. "Just remember that, Val."

"I'll remember," Val said. She walked away from Michelle, toward Kit, who was standing by the school's front door.

"Did you talk to him?" Kit asked. "I mean Rick."

"Why?" Val said. "Did Jamey say something to you?"

"Not about you," Kit said. "He talked about us instead. He asked if I wanted to go into the city with him Saturday. He said someone was doing *Juno and the Paycock* and it was about time we paid attention to my Irish roots. Then he mentioned brunch together on Sunday. I guess he's more worried about Mother than I realized."

"No," Val replied. "He's more worried about you."

"No reason to be," Kit said. "I'm all right."

"Kit, he loves you," Val said. "And he wants to spend some time with you. The way . . ."

"The way Rick spends times with you," Kit said. "Funny, Pop should be acting like this, with what's going on with you."

"Funny," Val said. "But okay."

"Yeah," Kit said. "It's okay." She smiled at Val. "He got home before supper last night," she said. "I asked him if he'd seen you, and he said yes, but he couldn't talk about it, so I didn't press him. Then we ate, and he drove us to the supermarket, so we could buy all the stuff we needed. We spent a fortune, but we had a really good time doing it. We put the groceries away together too, and we talked about me and school and what was going on in my life. Pop and I haven't talked like that since Mother began drinking again last spring. And then we had some ice cream and he mentioned the weekend, doing all those things together. I even told him about the mattress. He said we'd go shopping for a new one Saturday morning."

"That's great," Val said, and for the first time in her life, she envied Kit.

"It'll never last," Kit said. "But if we can just make it through the weekend, I'll be satisfied. So did you talk to Rick?"

Val shook her head. "I was too scared," she admitted.

"Rick can be scary," Kit replied. "You just never noticed before."

"I know I'm going to have to talk with him," Val said. "He thinks I'm acting strange anyway. He's right. I am. But I don't know what to say."

The school bell rang. "You'll think of something," Kit declared, which wasn't at all what Val wanted to hear. She sighed, and walked into the building with the other girls.

Val made it through the morning without too much trouble, but when the bell rang for her lunch period, she realized how much she dreaded going there. During class, no one could talk to her, and while she'd been aware the other girls were still looking at her far more than normal, she could at least pretend not to notice. But lunch meant conversations with nervous Michelle and happy Kit as well as the possibility of visits from people like Caroline, and Val didn't want to have anything to do with any of them. Besides, she wasn't hungry. So instead of going to the lunchroom, she slipped off to the library.

She put her books down, pleased at her choice of refuge, and stared for a moment out the window. Most Precious Blood was located on tree-covered grounds, and the leaves were changing their colors. Val thought about the evergreens at home and wondered what it would be like if they ever lost their leaves, and light would be allowed to shine into the house. It was safer to wonder about that than about what Rick would say to her when she confronted him with what she knew.

"Val?"

Val turned around and saw Sister Gina Marie standing by her side.

"Yes?" Val said.

"May I sit down?" Sister Gina Marie asked. "I looked for you in the lunchroom, and when I didn't see you, I thought I might find you in here."

Val nodded. Sister Gina Marie took the seat next to her. Sister Rosemary didn't even look up. Val supposed it was all right if one of the teachers made noise in the library.

"I've been worrying about you," Sister Gina Marie said. "Have you had a chance to talk with your father?"

Val laughed. "You're the third person who's asked me that today," she said. "Michelle and Kit and now you."

"We're all concerned about you," Sister Gina Marie replied. "That's natural enough."

"Michelle's more concerned about herself," Val said.

"And what Daddy'll do to her family if he finds out she's the one who told me."

"Do you think he would do something?" Sister Gina Marie asked. "Or is Michelle exaggerating?"

Val remembered back to second grade. The girls were all telling what their fathers did for a living. "My daddy's a businessman," Val had said proudly. "He owns a construction business and builds lots of buildings."

One of the girls, what was her name, she left at the end of that year, burst into laughter. "Your daddy's a gangster," she'd said. "He kills people. Everybody knows that."

"Stop that, Shannon!" Sister Anne had said. Shannon, that's right. Shannon O'Roarke. She and Kit had been friends in kindergarten until Shannon had failed to invite her to a birthday party.

"My daddy is not a gangster," Val had said. Had she cried? She thought she remembered crying. "What's a gangster?"

"A gangster is a bad man," Sister Anne had replied. "Your father is a respectable businessman. I want all you children to repeat after me, 'Mr. Castaladi is a respectable businessman.' "

They all had too. If Sister Anne had told them to say "Mr. Castaladi is a communist spy," they would have. Val didn't think she had reported the incident to her father when she'd gotten home, but she'd probably said something to her mother or to Connie. Or maybe Kit had, or Michelle. All Val knew was Shannon O'Roarke left Most Precious Blood, not at the end of the school year, now that she thought about it, but following Christmas vacation, and Rick gave the school a new stained-glass window for the chapel. The sisters made a big fuss about the window, and Val had been very proud of her daddy.

"Val? Are you all right?"

"I'm sorry," Val said. "I guess my mind wandered."

"I asked you if you'd had the chance to speak to your father," Sister Gina Marie said. "Or is he still in Washington?"

"He's back home," Val said. "He got in last night. But I haven't talked with him yet. Not about what Michelle told me."

It was hard to read Sister Gina Marie's reaction. Val thought at first she was concerned, but then she imagined she saw relief as well. Was Sister Gina Marie worried that Rick would hold Most Precious Blood responsible for her finding out? Had Sister Mary Margaret, the headmistress, talked with Sister Gina Marie about the consequences of Mr. Castaladi's displeasure? At the very least, Rick might insist that all the Castaladi relations, as well as the ones on Val's mother's side, leave the school. Val added the numbers rapidly in her mind. There were at least ten or twelve kids she was related to at Most Precious Blood, if you started with kindergarten, and probably an equal number at Sacred Heart. Rick wouldn't have to resort to violence to do damage to the school.

"Are you going to talk to him?" Sister Gina Marie asked.

"I don't know," Val replied. "What do you think I should do?"

Sister Gina Marie hesitated. "There are no easy answers," she replied. "I prayed for you last night, Val, hoping Our Lord would give you His guidance."

Nun talk. Val had hoped for better from Sister Gina Marie. "He didn't," she said.

"Maybe He has, but you just haven't heard Him," Sister Gina Marie replied. "Have you tried praying?"

Val shook her head.

"Then you might do better in the chapel than in the library," Sister Gina Marie said. "You might find your answers there."

"I know what I'll find there," Val said. "A stained-glass window my father paid for to show what a respectable businessman he is."

"I don't know your father," Sister Gina Marie said. "I met him once or twice last year at school functions, but that's been it. But I have no doubts he loves you very much, and I know you love him every bit as much."

"I'm glad you have no doubts," Val said. "Because I sure do."

"You're not a bitter girl," Sister Gina Marie said. "I've known you long enough to be sure of that."

"You've known me six weeks," Val said. "Since school began. How can you possibly claim you know me?"

Sister Gina Marie put her hand on Val's. "This is a very hard time for you," she said. "But there are many people who love you. They're praying you'll be able to work things out, and find peace again."

"I never had peace," Val said. "I had lies. Lies about who I was, who my father was. Lies even about my mother. I can't go back to those lies, and I can't imagine what I'm going ahead to. How much truth am I supposed to face?"

"God will be with you," Sister Gina Marie replied. "And He'll see to it you'll be surrounded by people who love you. Don't ever doubt that."

"I might have believed that a week ago," Val said. "A week ago, I believed just about everything I was told. A week ago, I didn't even question why I wasn't allowed to take a walk by myself. I don't believe anything anymore. If one thing in my life is a lie, then they all are. If I can't have faith in my father, why should I have faith in God?"

"Because faith in God comes first," Sister Gina Marie said. "All other belief stems from that."

Val shook her head. "Not in my world," she said. "In my world, belief starts with Rick Castaladi. What he tells you to believe is what you believe. If he decides there isn't any God, then there isn't. It's that simple."

"Nothing is that simple," Sister Gina Marie said. "Not even your father would claim that sort of power."

"What do you know about him?" Val asked. "Do you know something you haven't told me?"

Sister Gina Marie closed her eyes for a moment. "Belief begins with God," she said. "But answers begin with your father. You know you'll have to talk with him at some point."

"When I'm ready," Val said.

"I'll continue to pray for you," Sister Gina Marie said.

Val managed a smile. "Pray for my English grades while you're at it," she said. "How did I do on that quiz anyway?"

"You flunked it," Sister Gina Marie replied. "Along with just about everybody else."

"Even Kit?" Val asked.

"Kit's essay said nothing," Sister Gina Marie declared. "But she said it so beautifully, I couldn't bear to fail her."

"I'm glad," Val said. "Kit doesn't have much going for her right now, except for school."

"You're a good girl, Val," Sister Gina Marie said. "I know you're angry now, but basically you're sound. That's why I have so much faith you'll come through this crisis with your heart and your soul intact."

"I'm glad you think so, Sister," Val said. "Because you're the only one at this table who does."

Chapter 8

• • •

"**M**AY I COME home with you after school?" Val asked Kit at lunch on Thursday.

"Still avoiding Rick?" Kit asked.

Val nodded. She'd done fairly well the night before, mostly because Rick didn't get back until nine-thirty. But there was no reason to expect he'd be late that night, and that could mean a long evening of evasion.

"You can come over," Kit said. "But I'd better warn you. Pop's planning on coming home early and working in. He even said something about helping me make supper."

"Jamey?" Val said. Jamey once claimed he could burn water.

Kit laughed. "I think we'll end up ordering out," she said. "You're welcome to join us if you want."

Val thought about it. She was no more ready to socialize with Jamey than she was to confront her father. "Daddy wouldn't like it if I didn't have supper with him," she said. "We haven't really eaten together in days. But I'd still like to visit a little bit this afternoon."

"Fine," Kit said. "We can talk about my bedroom."

"What about your bedroom?" Val asked.

"Pop and I were talking about it last night," Kit replied. "And he said if I had to buy a new mattress, maybe I should get a new bed to go with it. And I kind of mentioned having outgrown the wallpaper, you know how Mother likes that little girly stuff for me, and Pop just laughed and said if I wanted, I could have my whole room redone while Mother was at the clinic. She's going to be there for at least a month, so there's plenty of time. I'd really like your help."

"What do I know about decorating?" Val asked, but she was pleased to be included.

"At least as much as Pop and I do," Kit said. "I thought you might want to ask Rick if you could redo your room too. We're sixteen now. It's about time our bedrooms looked it."

"I like my room," Val said. "I don't want to change it. Besides . . ."

"Besides what?" Kit asked.

Val wasn't sure how to put it. "I don't know where I'm going to end up," she finally said.

"Where do you think you're going to end up?" Kit asked. "At the orphan home? Rick's your father no matter how you started out. And he's going to stay your father for the rest of your life."

"Has Jamey said something to you?" Val asked. "About the adoption?"

"Not a word," Kit said. "But I've known you and Rick both long enough to know nothing bad's going to happen to you. Just talk to him, Val, and get it over with. I'm sure he has a perfectly reasonable explanation."

Val looked down at her lasagne. "What does Jamey say about him?" she asked. "When Daddy has a legal problem, I mean. What does Jamey tell you?"

"Nothing," Kit said. "He just works later hours."

"What does he tell Amanda then?" Val said. "When he thinks you aren't listening."

"Pop doesn't talk about his work," Kit replied. "Sometimes he'll say he had a hard day, or he'll mention having to deal with someone he doesn't like, but that's it. You want to find out about Rick's business, you're going to have to ask him directly."

"Do you remember when Sister Anne made us all say 'Mr. Castaladi is a respectable businessman'?" Val asked.

"Back in second grade?" Kit said. "Yeah, I remember."

"I thought about that yesterday," Val said. "About how Shannon O'Roarke left school so suddenly."

"Her father got transferred to Detroit," Kit said. "Kevin told me all about it when it happened. There were three or four O'Rourke kids, and Kevin was in the same grade as one of them. Kevin said Mr. O'Rourke got transferred to Detroit, and his wife didn't want to go, but Mr. O'Roarke said someone put a lot of pressure on his boss to see to it he got transferred someplace far away. And Kevin asked the O'Roarke kid why he was telling him that, and the kid said because Pop always did the dirty work . . ."

"For Rick Castaladi," Val said.

Kit nodded. "Kevin hates Pop," she said. "He has for as long as I can remember. He probably made the whole story up just so I'd hate Pop too."

"Kevin doesn't have that much imagination," Val said.

Kit looked around the lunchroom. "You don't want to talk about this here," she said. "Let's wait until we get to my house."

"Okay," Val said. Not that it mattered. Every girl at Most Precious Blood probably had a similar story to tell. No wonder there were so many houses she was excluded from. She felt so dirty right then, she agreed with all those righteous mothers.

She made it through the rest of the school day, and was glad when the final bell rang, and she could escape to Kit's. Bruno met them in front of the school grounds, and Val told him where to drive them.

"When you want to go home, be sure to call," Bruno said. "No more little walks, okay?"

"I'll call," Val said.

Kit laughed. Val was too peeved to ask what was so funny. Besides, she was sure she didn't want to hear the answer.

Kit unlocked the door, called to Bruno that everything was fine, and let Val in. Val noticed right away that the slashed paintings were gone.

"Pop took them to see if they could be repaired," Kit said, taking Val's jacket. "Sometimes canvas can be sewn."

"That would be great," Val said. "I miss those paintings."

"So does Pop," Kit replied. "But I'm not going to miss the wallpaper in my bedroom. Come on up. Let's analyze."

Val followed her friend upstairs. Kit's room was familiar and dear to her, but she knew she couldn't keep Kit from growing up. "What's that?" she asked, pointing to the bedroom door.

Kit blushed. "It's a lock," she said. "Pop had a locksmith come over yesterday to put it in. He was afraid if he postponed it, he'd forget."

"What do you need a lock for?" Val asked.

"In case Mother really goes crazy next time," Kit said. "Mistakes me for a mattress. You know."

Val sank onto the soon-to-be-replaced bed. "Amanda wouldn't do that," she said.

"I don't think so either," Kit replied. "But I wasn't

about to argue with Pop. Not when he was offering to redo my whole room. What do you think about yellow?"

"I like it," Val said. "Nice and cheerful."

"You don't think it's too cheerful, do you?" Kit asked. "I just haven't been feeling somber the past couple of days. But I might once Mother comes back. Maybe I should pick a lower-keyed color, just to be prepared."

"I'm glad one of us is happy," Val said.

"Hey, look," Kit said. "You want to play 'I suffer more than you do,' I'm ready."

"No," Val said, although it was a temptation. "I'm glad you're happy. I really am. How about a very soft yellow?"

"I like the sound of it," Kit said. "But what about the woodwork? And what color should my new bedspread be, and the curtains?"

The doorbell rang before Val could come up with an answer. "You expecting someone?" she asked.

Kit shook her head. "Want to come with me?"

"Okay," Val said. The two girls went downstairs, and Kit opened the door. When the doorbell rang at Val's house, Bruno or Connie always answered. Now that Val thought about it, she wasn't allowed to open the door by herself.

It was Malcolm. "Do you mind a surprise visitor?" he asked. "I thought since we didn't have that long to visit on Tuesday, I'd come on over today."

"I'm glad you did," Kit said. "Come on in. Val's here."

"I see," Malcolm said. "Hi, Val. How're things?"

"They're the same," Val said.

"Going with the status quo then," Malcolm said. "I don't blame you. Have you heard anything about your mother, Kit?"

"Pop talked to her doctors yesterday," Kit replied. "They

say she's a very sick woman." She smiled, but the joy was gone. "This is not a major revelation."

"Maybe this clinic is the answer," Malcolm said.

"Oh, Malcolm," Kit said. "It's the fifth rehab center in three years."

Val had a strong and unpleasant feeling of being excluded. It wasn't right. She'd known Amanda a lot longer than Malcolm had, even if they were related. And before Malcolm came, she and Kit were managing just fine, actually having a good time. Kit must know it was a fool's paradise, but that didn't mean she couldn't enjoy it while it lasted.

"How about something to drink?" Kit asked. "This time I have ginger ale and everything."

"Sounds good," Malcolm said.

"I don't think so," Val said. "I should probably be going home now."

"So soon?" Kit asked.

Val nodded. "I have a lot of homework to do," she said. "And a French test tomorrow. I'll call Bruno and ask him to pick me up."

"All right," Kit said.

Val walked over to the telephone and dialed her home number. She got a busy signal. "Busy," she told them. "I don't feel like waiting. I'll just walk home."

"You know you can't do that," Kit said.

"Why not?" Malcolm asked. "Is it too far?"

"She isn't allowed," Kit replied. "And if she does, then Rick'll get mad at me for not making her wait."

"Do you think something bad'll happen?" Val asked. "Do you think Jamey'll suddenly be transferred to Detroit?"

"All I think is you should wait a few minutes, and try calling again," Kit said.

"No," Val said. "I want to go home now."

"I'll drive you," Malcolm said.

"Malcolm," Kit said. "You don't have to do that."

"No, it's all right," he said. "I'll come back here, once I see Val's safely home."

Kit was silent for a moment. "All right," she said. "But don't take too long, okay?"

It angered Val that Kit was so eager to have Malcolm to herself. She obviously wanted him around because he was a relative, he was blood. In years past, that wouldn't have bothered her nearly so much. She could always go to Michelle, or some other Castaladi. But now she had no one, and Kit didn't even seem to care.

She barely said goodbye to Kit, and didn't open her mouth again until Malcolm had begun driving away. She wouldn't have spoken then, if he hadn't asked her a question.

"You and Kit have a fight?" he asked.

"No," she said. "I just think she could be a little more sensitive to my needs."

"Kit has a lot on her mind right now," Malcolm said.

"I know that," Val said. "She reminds me all the time. But I'm the one who just found out she was adopted. You'd think that would count for something."

"Kit's worried about you," Malcolm said. "I called her yesterday to see how things were going, and she told me what was happening with you. But right now, she's trying to get her own life in order."

"She's trying to pretend her mother's dead," Val said. "She and Jamey are acting like Amanda doesn't exist anymore. It makes me sick. My mother is dead, well I thought she was my mother, and I miss her all the time." She fell silent for a moment, as she realized that was true. She thought she'd stopped missing her mother long ago, but ever since she'd opened her mother's secret shoe-box, she'd found herself longing for her mother's touch, the sound of her voice, the way she knew how to comfort when it seemed that nothing could lessen the pain.

But Malcolm didn't know Val well enough to understand her silence. "I know you're going through a very rough time," he said. "But Kit seems sure things are going to work out for you. And she needs this time away from Amanda. The second time I was over there for dinner, Amanda got stinking drunk, and it was terrifying. I've seen people drunk before, but never like that."

"Kit's used to it," Val said.

Malcolm shook his head. "You don't ever get used to that kind of anger," he said. "Even Jamey was scared."

I'm scared too, Val thought, but she didn't say it. "My house is the next block down," she said instead. "The one in the middle with the fence."

"I see it," Malcolm said. He drove in front of it and parked.

"Thank you," Val said. "Goodbye."

"I'll come in with you," Malcolm said.

"You don't have to," Val said.

"I think I'd better," Malcolm replied. "In case Kit asks." He got out of the car and watched as Val unlatched the gate.

"Connie'll probably ask you to stay," Val said. "But I know you want to get back to Kit."

"That's all right," Malcolm said. "I'm just making sure you get home safely."

Val unlocked the front door. But before she had the chance to open it completely, her father did it for her.

"Valentina," he said. "How did you get home?"

"I got a ride," Val said. Did he have to call her that

stupid name? And in front of Malcolm, who had probably thought she was named Valerie or something else equally as sensible.

"From who?" Rick asked.

"From me," Malcolm said. "I don't think we've been introduced. I'm Malcolm Scott."

"Malcolm Scott," Rick said. "What kind of a name is that?"

"Make a wild guess," Malcolm said. "Well, Val, I've left you safely in the arms of your bodyguard. I might as well get going."

"Bodyguard!" Rick said. "I'm no bodyguard. I'm her father."

"Whoops," Malcolm said. "Sorry. It's a pleasure to meet you, Mr. Castaladi, but I really have to go now."

"Wait one second, young man," Rick said.

"Daddy," Val said.

Rick ignored her. "How do you know my daughter?" he asked. "Do you go to Sacred Heart?"

"I'm not even Catholic," Malcolm said.

"You're not?" Rick said. "Val, go to your room at once."

"Daddy, stop it," Val said. "Malcolm's Kit's cousin. That's all."

"Her cousin?" Rick asked.

Malcolm nodded. "My mother and Amanda are sisters," he said. "I was over at Kit's, and Val wanted to go home, and she called here and got a busy signal, so I offered to drive her. I didn't realize I had to be a Catholic to give a girl a lift."

"I don't care for funny business," Rick said. "Not if my daughter's involved."

"I understand, and I don't blame you," Malcolm said.

"And I truly am sorry about that bodyguard crack. It's just where I come from, Indiana, sixteen-year-old girls walk home by themselves all the time. I guess customs are different here."

"I'm sorry too," Rick said, and he no longer looked like he wanted to take a swing at Malcolm. "It was very nice of you to give my daughter a lift. But I'm sure you understand my concern when I see her coming home with a strange boy."

"Not really," Malcolm said. "That's another thing sixteen-year-old girls do in Indiana."

Rick smiled. "I think we've established that we're not in Indiana," he declared. "Now I'm sure you want to get back to Kit."

"Very much so," Malcolm said. "Goodbye, Val. I think I understand now."

"Goodbye, Malcolm," Val said, not sure whether she wanted to laugh or cry. Malcolm didn't wait to see what she would do, and her father slammed the door the minute Malcolm began walking away.

"Valentina Castaladi, I think we have some talking to do," her father said.

"Don't call me that," Val said. She hung her jacket up in the hall closet, then flung her schoolbooks down.

"And don't use that tone of voice with me," Rick said. "Do you care to tell me what's going on?"

"Nothing's going on," Val said. "Everything's just fine."

"I've never laid a hand on you," Rick said. "But you're not too old for me to start."

"Sure," Val said. "That's your answer for everything, isn't it, Daddy. When you don't know how else to handle something, there's always brute force."

"Is it your hormones?" Rick asked. "Your mother sometimes got like this, angry and raw, at her time of month."

"Leave my mother out of it!" Val cried. "And this has nothing to do with my hormones. I don't even have my period. I lied to you about that."

"You lied?" Rick said. "Since when have I ever been so cruel to you, you had to lie?"

"There are lots of different ways of being cruel," Val declared. "You'd be surprised how many of them you know." She turned her back to her father, and began walking up the stairs.

"Stop, right now!" Rick shouted, and Val was too scared not to. "You come back here and tell me what's going on. Something's been wrong since Monday, and I demand an explanation."

Val laughed. "You want an explanation?" she said. "Not half as much as I do, Daddy." The word sounded poisonous to her.

"I don't know what you're talking about," Rick said. "I don't owe you any explanations."

"Is that what you told Mama?" Val asked. "When you did whatever you felt like doing."

"Your mother never asked me for explanations," Rick said. "She knew I told her only what she needed to know. The rest she was just as happy not to hear. That's how it is with husbands and wives. You'll learn that soon enough."

"You're crazy," Val said. "I'm never going to be like Mama. And I'm certainly never going to marry a man like you."

"Don't make me hit you," Rick said.

"I don't care if you do," Val replied. "You can do whatever you want to me, and it won't matter."

"Go to your room," Rick said. "I'm calling the doctor. I think you must be very sick."

"There's nothing wrong with me, Daddy," Val said. "I'm not Mama. There's nothing eating away at me, except disgust for you."

"You heard me," Rick said. "Go to your room."

Val shook her head. "I don't care what you say to me. I don't care what you do. You can throw me out of this house, and that's fine with me. You don't count any more, Daddy. You stopped counting the moment I found out the truth."

"What truth?" Rick asked. "What the hell are you talking about?"

"You know what truth I mean," Val said. "The truth you've been keeping from me for sixteen years now." She stared at the face of the man she'd always thought of as her father, and no longer saw anger there, but pain and confusion and hopeless love. "Oh, Daddy!" she cried. "If I'm not a Castaladi, then who am I?"

Chapter 9

• • •

HAT?"

Val grabbed onto the bannister. "I know I'm adopted," she said. "I found out, Daddy."

Rick stood absolutely still, then slowly nodded.

"I have to learn what happened," Val said. "It's tearing me up, not knowing."

"We need to talk," her father said. "Not here, not with you on the staircase. Let's go into the den."

Val followed him into the den. Of all the dark rooms in the house, it was the darkest, with evergreens blocking all the sun from the windows. Rick automatically turned the overhead light on and, almost as automatically, closed the door. He sat down on the sofa and beckoned Val to join him, but she chose a chair instead.

"I don't know how to handle this," Rick said. "I honestly thought this would never happen."

"I have so many questions," Val said. "Am I your daughter?"

Rick sighed. "Of course you are," he replied. "I love you, I take care of you, I'm proud of you. But I'm not your father in the way you mean."

"So I'm not a Castaladi," Val said. She felt some sense

of relief that she wasn't the product of an adulterous affair or even of a surrogate arrangement. "All these years, you've been lying to me."

"There are a lot of ways we can handle this," Rick said. "You can ask questions, or I can simply tell you the story, or you can fling accusations at me. You get to pick, but choose wisely. I may never be this open again."

"I'm angry," Val said.

Rick laughed. "That's obvious," he replied. "Tell me, how did you find out?"

"I was looking through Mama's things while you were gone," Val said. "And I found a letter she wrote me when she was dying. She wrote all about how she couldn't have a baby, and how you brought her one as a gift."

"Neither one of us wanted you to know," Rick said. "I guess being sick for so long, knowing she was going to die, it did things to her mind. I wish she'd talked to me about it. I would have told her not to write that letter."

"I'm glad she did," Val said. "I have a right to know."

"Are you happier knowing?" her father asked. "Is your world a better place for knowing?"

"That's not fair," Val said. "It's only been a couple of days, and I've had a lot more questions than answers. Ask me again in twenty years."

"You're right," Rick said, strumming his fingers on the arm of the sofa. "Just understand, we only wanted to protect you."

"You're always protecting me, Daddy," Val said. "I don't know from what though."

"I have enemies," he said. "A man in my position always does. My father had them, my brother has them. Enemies don't always check bloodlines. It's better to be overly cautious."

"What are my bloodlines?" Val asked. "Do you know?"

"Of course I know," her father replied. "What kind of question is that? Do you think I'd take some strange child into my house, raise her as my own?"

"I don't know what I know anymore," Val said. "Tell me who I am."

"You're Valentina Maria Castaladi," Rick said. "Daughter of Richard and Barbara Castaladi. Are you so determined to find out all the rest?"

"Yes," Val said. "I am."

"And what if you don't like it?" he asked. "You've had a couple of days to make up a brand-new heritage for yourself. I know what girls are like. You probably think you're the daughter of kings and queens, or your mother was a movie star, or your father some big millionaire."

"I haven't thought anything," Val said. "I've been too scared to think."

"And what were you so scared of?" Rick asked. "The truth? Me?"

Val nodded. She yearned to cry, but knew if she did, Rick would close up, and she would never learn what she needed. So she clenched her hand into a fist until her fingernails cut into her flesh. The pain focused her. "Tell me everything," she said. "I don't want to be scared anymore."

"Everything," Rick said. "You ask for a lot."

"If you don't, I won't be able to love you," Val replied. "And I want to, Daddy."

"All right," Rick said. "Everything. I suppose that starts when I married your mother. Our families had done business together for years. Everyone supposed I'd marry Barbara's older sister, Ann Marie, but she died, and there was Barbara. Pretty girl, and sweet. I'd always liked her more than Ann Marie, so it all worked out fine as far as I was concerned. I was a few years older, but that was all right too. She looked up to me, and that's what a husband wants. A wife who respects and honors him."

"Mama said there was some trouble," Val declared. "That the two of you were engaged for a long time because of some trouble."

"She wrote that?" Rick asked. "About the trouble?"

Val nodded.

"It was nothing," he said. "A little mixup concerning my poppa's business. I was in jail for a few months before his lawyers got it taken care of. I guess it was important to Barbara though, since it meant we had to wait a while before we could be married."

"I thought you never went to jail," Val said. "I've even bragged about it."

"It was years ago," Rick said. "A mistake. I was in maybe six months before it got straightened out."

"Were you guilty?" Val asked.

"You have a choice here," Rick said. "You can ask me about my prison record, and I can explain all the details to you, or we can go on with the story of how you became my daughter. Which do you prefer?"

"Go on," Val said with a sigh.

"Fine," her father said. "I married Barbara. Big affair, lots of guests, lots of dancing. Everything she had dreamed of. We went to the Virgin Islands on our honeymoon." He paused for a moment, and looked out the window. Val knew the only view he had was of the past. "We had a real nice time," he finally said. "Barbara was everything I wanted in a wife. And she loved me. That was a very special time. But we came home, everybody started teasing us right away, where's the baby, what's a honeymoon for if not making babies. Only she wasn't pregnant. And she didn't get pregnant. After a while, the jokes stopped, but the questions never did. What were we waiting for? Was everything all right? This went on for years. For years we lied to ourselves, said everything was fine. Then finally I insisted Barbara have tests. Maybe it was some little problem that could be fixed. We'd be better off knowing. Barbara knew that was true, but she was terrified of what the tests would say. But she obeyed me and saw the doctors."

"What did they say?" Val asked.

"They said nothing to her," Rick replied. "To me they said there was nothing wrong, nothing they could find. I knew what had to be done. So I saw a doctor too, and had tests run, and it wasn't Barbara's fault that there weren't any babies. I was the one with the problem, and it was a problem they couldn't fix."

"Mama thought it was her fault," Val said. "Her letter never said it was yours."

"I never told her," Rick declared. "She would have lost all respect for me if she knew I couldn't father a son. She might have left me, and what would I have told people? The only one who knew was my poppa. To him I confided everything. My poppa was a great man. I was his favorite, although I wasn't the oldest. I followed his guidance. He said Barbara must never know, that nobody should know. Barbara's cousin Connie couldn't bear children, and Barbara's family was weak anyway, everyone knew that, so it was natural to assume the problem was hers. He asked me if Barbara would be happier knowing I was the reason she had no babies. Of course the answer was no. So I kept the truth from her, and it was just as well. She was sickly, the same as her sisters, and if she had left me, married some other man, just to have babies, who knows. She might have died in childbirth. My poppa said it was not for us to question the ways of God, and he was right."

Val tried to picture her mother, but it hurt too much. She looked at the TV set instead. There was a picture of the three of them there, taken on Val's eleventh birthday. That was the last good time Val could remember them sharing.

"I felt since it was my fault Barbara couldn't have a baby, it was my responsibility to bring her one," Rick said. "She was a good woman, and she asked for so little. I asked Poppa how I could do this, get a baby for her, and he asked his lawyers. They said we could never go through an agency, because of that jail business, and who I was. I got angry then. I wasn't in Poppa's business. My brother Mike, as the first born, had been taken in, and Poppa had helped me set up my construction business, which was going great. I had this big empty house, a loving wife, and a successful business, and some damnfool agency was going to deny me a baby because my name was Castaladi. A name to be proud of. I told Poppa how I felt, and he asked the lawyers what would happen if he applied a little muscle to an agency, but they said that would be a mistake, and there were other ways of getting babies and they'd look into them."

"Gray market," Val said. "I know someone who was adopted that way."

Rick nodded. "The lawyers said it could take time, and I was impatient. There were other problems too. It was bad enough the only way I could give Barbara a child was by adoption. It couldn't be a son. A daughter, I knew I could live with. What does a man care about a daughter?

They're for loving, for dressing pretty, for giving you grandchildren. They bear your name only until they're married. A son would be a Castaladi. He'd expect to take over the business. I couldn't accept that if he wasn't my blood. With gray market, the girl might have a boy, and still expect us to adopt. Or she might change her mind, and if we put any pressure on her to live up to her end of the bargain, she might make a stink about it. And she might not be Italian, or even Catholic. It was too chancy. I wanted a baby girl as close to me as I could get. I told Poppa this, and he agreed."

"So what did you do?" Val asked.

Her father laughed. "I waited," he said. "There wasn't much else I could do. And I had Poppa tell his people to be on the lookout for a baby girl that fit the description. But it was Poppa himself who found you. I knew when I placed my trust in him, he wouldn't fail me. He always came through for me, and this time was no exception."

"How?" Val asked.

"Papa's grandfather had a sister," Rick replied. "Rosa Castaladi. She married into the Primo family, had six or seven kids. The Primos were garbage, always letting people know they were part Castaladi, but never amounting to anything. Poppa mostly heard from the Primos when they needed a favor. They were never close-knit, not like the Castaladis. Some moved to Vegas, some to Chicago. One branch moved to Buffalo. That was Donny Primo. He had a wife, a few kids. His son Charley married Carmela Rinaldi. They asked Poppa to be godfather to one of their boys. Otherwise I don't think Poppa would have even remembered they were alive. That branch of the Rinaldis frankly wasn't much better than the Primos. It was a good match though. Carmela was healthy, gave him three sons, a couple of daughters."

"Am I one of those daughters?" Val asked.

Rick raised his hand to shush her. "Charley Primo got a job like Bruno's," he said. "For Gino Petrolli, a very big person in upstate New York. Charley was not a real bright guy, but they figured he could drive a car and make sure everything was safe. It turned out this was a little more than Charley could handle. There was some trouble in Buffalo with the Conti family, a little bit of warfare, and Charley ended up in the line of fire along with Gino Petrolli. Unfortunately, it turned out Charley's mother was part Conti, and he hadn't bothered to tell anyone that. No one said he was to blame, after all he'd been killed along with Gino, but the Petrollis didn't feel any responsibility to Carmela and the kids. Poppa was informed because of the Castaladi connection. He made a couple of phone calls to Buffalo to see what the situation was, and found out Carmela had had a baby girl a month or so before. A few more phone calls were made, to make sure the baby was healthy and normal, and then Poppa himself went to Buffalo to talk to Carmela."

"Did she want to give the baby up?" Val asked. It was easier to think of it as "the baby," than to identify it as herself.

"She had six kids," Rick replied. "The oldest was maybe fourteen. The Primo family had no money, that part of the Rinaldis weren't much better off. The Petrollis were offering nothing, and she didn't dare turn to the Contis. I'm sure she loved the baby very much, but she could see that giving her up was the best for everybody. Certainly the best for the little girl. She didn't agree right away, but Poppa made her see the light. It was all completely legal.

Poppa called me at my office, told me the baby was mine if I wanted it, and I said yes, sight unseen. Poppa flew the baby down. I met him at the airport, took the baby, and drove it to my house, to give to Barbara."

"And that was me," Val said.

"You were a pretty little kid," Rick said. "I could see you were okay, healthy and all that. And Poppa reminded me you were part Castaladi, part my blood. But I didn't feel anything for you, not at first. Poppa did. He loved you as much, maybe more, than any of his other grandkids. And Barbara. You should have seen her face light up when I gave you to her. It was like all those years of trying and failing just vanished. She had a baby. She asked if she could name you Valentina, because you must have been born right around Valentine's Day, and I said sure. I didn't care. For a long time, I hated you, Val, because to have you in my house was a constant reminder of my own failure, that I would never have a son, a true heir. I asked Poppa what I should do, if I kept on hating you, and he laughed and said no one could keep hating a baby. He was right. One day you crawled to me and looked right at me with so much love in your eyes I knew it didn't matter if you were blood or not, you were my daughter. I picked you up that day, and when you hugged me, it was electric, and from that moment on, you were truly my child."

"Oh, Daddy," Val said.

"That's the story," Rick said. "Of course everyone knew you were adopted, but they were all sworn to secrecy. Poppa kept it to himself that you were a Primo. They weren't a family held in wide regard, and besides, with that business about the Contis, we both felt it was best if no one knew."

"My mother," Val said. "Carmela. Do you know what became of her?"

"She's still in Buffalo," Rick replied. "She could tell you where all your brothers and sisters are, if you want to know."

"I need to see her, Daddy," Val said. "I'm sorry, but I do."

"And when you see her, what happens then?" Rick asked. "You move in with her, become a Primo? You forget all the years you've lived here, all the love we've shared?"

"No, of course not," Val said, although truthfully, she had no idea what would happen. "I know you're my father. I know Mama was my mother. But I'm not going to feel complete unless I see her. I hope you can understand that."

"It's always blood," Rick said. "That need to know exactly where you belong. I understand. I'll call Carmela if you want, make arrangements with her so you can see her this weekend. Do you want her to come down here?"

Val knew that was what Rick wanted, so he could at least have some control over the reunion. But she also knew there were a lot of unanswered questions she never would have the courage to ask under his roof. "No," she said. "I think I should go to Buffalo. If I'm going to see where I came from, I should see it as it really is."

"All right," Rick said. "Maybe that is better. Otherwise you might have some illusions I snatched you from a palace."

"I don't think I have any illusions," Val said. "Not anymore."

"We'll go on Saturday," Rick said. "Do you think you can hold out until then?"

"We?" Val said.

"We," Rick said. "You and me."

"No, Daddy," Val said. "I can't go with you."

"Why not?" Rick demanded. "You think I've been feeding you lies? You think you'll go up to Buffalo, meet this woman, and find out I snatched you from her breast?"

"I don't think that," Val said.

"Fine," Rick said. "So the two of us will go together. You want some time alone with Carmela, I'll wait in another room."

Val shook her head. "I won't go with you," she declared.

"Then you won't go," Rick said.

"And then what?" Val asked. "I'll snipe at you, the way I have been? I'll go out with boys you don't approve of? I'll give Bruno the slip, start staying out late, run away from home?" She tried to remember Jamey's list. "Alcohol, drugs, pregnancy? Just because I'm angry?"

"Then don't be angry," Rick said. "Obey your father, the way you were brought up to. Be a good girl, go to school, meet the right boy, and have a beautiful wedding. What's wrong with that?"

"Nothing," Val said. "Except it won't work anymore."

"I don't see that anything's changed," Rick replied. "You've agreed, I'm still your father. You're still my daughter, my Valentina. I know you're confused right now, but you're still a good girl, and you know you should obey me."

Val wished she could be angry again. Things were simpler when rage dictated her moves. "Obedience is based on trust," she said. "And I can't trust you anymore. Maybe I will again, but not now. Not after I find out you've been lying to me for my entire life. If you'd found that out, found out someone you loved had lied to you for sixteen years, could you trust them again right away?"

"We never lied," Rick said. "We kept things from you, that's all."

"You lied to me about jail," Val said. "You always told me you'd never been in jail, and now it turns out you were."

"That was a mistake," Rick replied. "I shouldn't have spent a single day there."

"But you did," Val said. "Daddy, you know you've been lying."

"I know I don't care for this tone," Rick said.

"What are you going to do about it?" Val asked. "Give me amnesia for the past week? Make like none of it ever happened? We can't go back to that. Maybe it would have been better if I never found out, but I did. And I need to meet her, to meet Carmela, and I can't do it with you waiting in the hallway for me."

"Fine," Rick said. "Have it your way. I'll send you up with Bruno instead."

"No," Val said. "Not Bruno."

"You can't go alone," Rick declared. "I forbid that."

Val hated the idea that her father felt he could still forbid things, but she also knew he was right. She was terrified to fly to Buffalo alone. She wouldn't even know how. Her sole experience of traveling alone had been the walk home from Jamey's office two days earlier.

"Jamey," she said. "I'll go with him." She liked the idea of his lawyerly presence.

"And Bruno," Rick said. "In case the Petrollis have a long memory."

Val realized then how many lies there had been, and how many things she had now to be frightened of. "There isn't any danger," she said.

"There's always danger," Rick replied. "Someone like Bruno just makes things a little safer."

"All right," Val said. "Jamey and Bruno. And we go on Saturday."

"I'll make the arrangements now," Rick said. "But, Val, promise me you'll remember none of that is what counts. What counts is you're my daughter."

"I promise," Val said. She got up from the chair, and although part of her wanted to go to Rick and kiss him, she found she couldn't. Instead she left the room and went upstairs to her bedroom.

The phone rang almost as soon as she got there. Val picked it up.

"Hi, Val? This is Malcolm. Kit gave me your number. I hope that's okay."

"It's okay," Val said.

"I'm just calling to apologize for leaving so abruptly," he said. "I guess, well, to be perfectly honest, your father scared me."

"Yes," Val said. "He has that effect on people sometimes."

"But everything's all right?" Malcolm asked. "I didn't make things worse?"

"Everything's all right," Val said. She couldn't even be sure if that was true. The truth was a dark muddy field, and lies cast a false light to be guided by.

Chapter 10

• • •

KIT WASN'T AT school the next day. Just like her, Val thought, to be sick the one day she was really needed. But having her missing made it easier for Val to concentrate on classes, on her French test, on the thousand little things that constituted education.

Michelle was there and, perhaps because Kit wasn't, had lunch for the first time with Val since their fight. Val was glad for the company, although she wasn't ready to confide in her cousin.

"Mama's still mad at me," Michelle said. "She thinks you're going to tell Rick and blame everything on me."

"I won't," Val said. I haven't, she thought.

"I said you wouldn't," Michelle replied. "I said we can trust you, you'd never want to hurt us. I said no matter what, you were my cousin. I don't care if your father's the king of England, you're still blood as far as I'm concerned."

"My father isn't king of England," Val said. "I think we can both be pretty sure about that."

"You know that I mean," Michelle said. "You still do think of me as your cousin, don't you?"

"Of course I do," Val said. "What about you?"

"I heard about the adoption business years ago," Michelle said. "Before your mother died. I've been a cousin to you all that time, haven't I?"

"I didn't know you could keep secrets that well," Val said.

"I wish I'd kept this one a little better," Michelle replied. "I'm really sorry, Val. I know this has been hard on you."

"It'll work out," Val said. "It just needs some time."

Michelle nodded. "If you need me, I'm here," she said. "Even if it's just to get mad at."

Val laughed. "We do that really well, don't we," she said. "Get mad at each other."

"You're like a sister to me that way," Michelle said. "Driving me crazy all the time."

Val took Michelle's hand and gave it a squeeze. "Hey," she said. "If you aren't my cousin, you might as well be my sister."

"Deal," Michelle said. "Now cut the crap, Sis, before I start crying."

For the first time that week, Val didn't dread gym class.

She missed Kit during English though, and especially wished she were there when Sister Gina Marie asked her to stay after for a few minutes.

"I really can't stay long" Val said. "I have a lot of things I have to do this afternoon."

"Just a moment then," Sister Gina Marie said. "I just want to find out how you're doing."

"I'm fine," Val said.

"And how are things with your father?" Sister Gina Marie asked.

Val thought about their strained breakfast together. They'd spoken only a few words, and both of them had been relieved when it was time for Bruno to drive Val to school. "He's under a lot of pressure," Val said. "He had to leave Washington early this week, and he's having labor troubles in Hackensack."

"That wasn't what I was asking about," Sister Gina Marie said.

"I really appreciate your concern," Val said. "But the only reason you feel involved is because you overheard what Michelle said. Michelle and I are okay now, and Daddy and I are going to be, and there's no more reason for you to worry."

"I can't just stop worrying," Sister Gina Marie said. "I have some idea of what you're going through, Val, and I know how hard it is."

"You can't possibly know," Val said. "Not unless you're adopted too."

Sister Gina Marie shook her head.

"Then don't say you know," Val said. "Because you don't. Half the time I don't even know, and I'm going through it."

"All right," Sister Gina Marie said. "But I do feel involved, and I want you to know it. And if you want to talk to me at any time, I'd be more than happy."

"Thank you," Val said. "What I'd really like to do is check up on Kit. So if you'll excuse me."

"Certainly," Sister Gina Marie said. "Tell her I hope she's feeling better."

Val nodded. She gathered her books and jacket and ran downstairs. She could see Bruno waiting for her. "Take me to Kit's," she said.

"I didn't see her," Bruno said.

"She was out," Val said. "I'm going now to see how she is."

"I'll wait for you," Bruno said.

Val knew that was a command, and she was in no position to fight it. "All right," she said. If Bruno had nothing better to do than sit around in the car waiting for her, that was his business. He'd be doing plenty of waiting around in Buffalo. He might as well get used to it.

Bruno kept his watchful eye on Val as she walked to Kit's front door. She rang the bell, and waited a few moments until Kit let her in.

"Are you all right?" Val asked. "I was worried about you when you weren't in school today."

"I'm okay," Kit said. "Come into the living room. My room's a mess. I've been there all day, and I didn't think I'd have company."

"I'm not company," Val said, sitting on the sofa. "What's the matter? Why weren't you in school?"

"It all just hit me," Kit said. "This whole week. Pop and I had a huge fight last night, and now that I have a lock on my bedroom door, I used it. I locked myself in, and I stayed there until he went to work this morning." She pulled her robe tighter around her pajamas, and for an instant she looked more like Amanda than she did Jamey.

Val thought about the real reason why she'd come over, to tell Kit everything her father had told her the day before. But she knew she'd have to get Kit's business out of the way first, so they could both concentrate on everything that was happening in Val's life.

"I didn't know you and Jamey fought," she said. "Not like that."

"We don't," Kit said. "It's really been a lousy week."

"But why?" Val asked. "I thought things were going well for you. Yesterday all you could talk about was redoing your bedroom. It was going to be yellow to match your mood. Did something happen with Amanda?"

Kit shook her head. "Not the way you think," she said. "Pop spoke to her doctor again, and we're supposed to go up next weekend and have one of those confrontational sessions. You know, we all make lists of how her drinking has hurt us. I'll just get my last list out and update it."

"You'll have a lot to put on," Val said.

"Just the mattress," Kit replied. "I'll spare her the rest. She's probably blacked it out anyway."

"If it wasn't Amanda, what did you and Jamey fight about?" Val asked.

Kit kicked her slippers off and sat cross-legged on the chair. "You really don't want to know," she said.

"It isn't a question of want," Val said. "You're always there when I need you. I just think I should be there for you too."

"Thank you," Kit said. "No, I mean that. Just because I'm mad at Pop and Rick too doesn't mean I should be mad at you."

"What does Daddy have to do with this?" Val asked.

"Remember all those wonderful plans Pop and I had for the weekend?" Kit asked. "Well, he cancelled. He got a phone call from your father last night, and the next thing I know he's telling me he has to go out of town on Saturday. He said I should see if Malcolm would go with me instead. I don't know why that made me so mad, the way he used Malcolm as a substitute, but I just started thinking about what that O'Roarke kid said about how Rick had Pop do his dirty work for him, and now Pop was trying to get Malcolm to do his, and I thought about all the reasons Kevin hates Pop, and how I'd never listen to him, never agree with him, but maybe he was right. I thought about it all in just the flash of a second, everything Pop's ever done for Rick, everything he's ever given up for him, and the list was so long, it made the list of things Mother's done just shrivel in comparison."

"Kit, there's an explanation," Val said, horribly aware she was the explanation.

"I'm tired of explanations," Kit declared. "I'm tired of protecting Mother from Pop and Pop from Mother. I'm tired of having an older brother I can't count on because he packed his bags and left when he was twelve. I'm tired of having a mother who's a hideous, miserable drunk, and I'm tired of having the Irish kids at Most Precious Blood look down their noses at me and the Italian kids think I'm weird. Mostly I'm tired of Pop, because I think he's responsible for a lot of things he's never been willing to claim responsibility for. Including me."

"Jamey loves you," Kit said. "He told me so just this week."

Kit shook her head. "Maybe he does," she said. "But it doesn't matter. Rick comes first with him. Anything Rick wants, Pop does. Kevin's told me for years how dirty the dealings are, the bribes, the kickbacks. Using third-rate materials at first-rate prices."

"I don't want to hear this," Val said.

"Sorry," Kit said. "We all come to grips with our fathers at different times. This week is my time. I thought maybe it was yours."

"Jamey isn't perfect," Val said. "Daddy certainly isn't. And you're right. I have been coming to grips with that this week. But nobody else is perfect either."

"You don't understand," Kit said. "I can't expect you to. But when Sister Anne made all of us say that about your father, about how he was a respectable businessman, I wanted her to make them say it about Pop too. Nobody ever teased you, because half of them thought Rick was perfectly okay, and the other half were scared stiff of him, of you, of everything the name Castaladi stands for. Farrell doesn't stand for anything, so I was an easy target."

"You're right," Val said. "I don't understand. You're sitting around in your robe at four in the afternoon because kids used to tease you when you were seven? That's crazy."

"I'm sitting around in my robe because I want a different set of parents," Kit replied. "I want a mother who isn't so lost and angry that all she can do is drink. I want a father who loves me more than he loves his boss. I want Pop once in his life to say to Rick, 'Sorry, but I have plans for Saturday. I'm spending the day with my daughter.' And you know something, I'd take all the rest, cleaning up after Mother, and everyone's attitude at school, all of it, if he'd just say that once, that I'm more important than work."

"This is all just a huge misunderstanding," Val said. "It wasn't Daddy that made Jamey change his plans."

"What do you mean, it wasn't Rick?" Kit asked. "Everything was set until Rick called."

"But he called for me," Val said. "I'm the one who asked for Jamey. I'm the one who needs him."

"What the hell are you talking about?" Kit asked.

Val smiled. "Daddy and I had it out yesterday," she said. "I guess it was a good day for father-daughter confrontations. He told me all about the adoption. It's fine, Kit. I mean I don't exactly come from royalty, but I come from a perfectly okay family. I'm even part Castaladi, if you look hard enough. My father was killed when I was an infant, and my mother didn't have any money, and there were lots of other kids, and Daddy wanted to adopt, so it all just worked out. There's more to the story than that, but those are the important details."

"Are you okay about it?" Kit asked.

"I'm not sure yet," Val said. "Mostly I feel relief that all those horrible explanations everyone kept coming up with weren't true. And you're right. There are things about Daddy's business that I haven't wanted to face. I like the idea that he's a respectable businessman. I've never wanted to think of him as anything else, and maybe I'm going to have to. But not this week. This week I've had enough to deal with."

Kit nodded. "It can wait," she said. "I guess for you, it'll have to."

"Daddy and I did our share of screaming yesterday," Val said. "Malcolm got us started when he drove me home, but I'm glad, because if something hadn't forced the issue, I might never have had the nerve to ask. I kept hoping it would all go away, but I'd remember things, like Shannon O'Roarke, and I was scared. You know how scared I was. And Jamey was no help, but he did keep telling me to ask Daddy, and when I did, I could see Jamey was right. That's why I thought of him, just because he is Daddy's lawyer, and he sees things differently than we do."

"You thought of him for what?" Kit asked.

"For going with me to Buffalo tomorrow," Val replied. "That's where she lives. My mother, I mean. The woman who gave birth to me. I'll always think of Mama as my mother, but this other woman lives in Buffalo. Daddy knew right away where she was, and I guess he called her and told her I wanted to go there. He said he would, that he'd take care of all the details, and I don't think he would have called Jamey unless he had. Daddy wanted to go with me, only I said no. I've never said no to him, not about anything serious, and we had a fight over that too, but I won. So then he said I had to go with Bruno, and I knew I'd need someone, but not Bruno. Have you ever had a real conversation with Bruno? You could fall asleep trying. So I thought of Jamey, and the way he listens when you talk to him, and the way he really seems to understand. I've always loved that about him. He never acts like you're a kid."

"No," Kit said. "He acts like you're a client."

"Which is just what I want," Val said. "I want my lawyer with me. I'm going to meet this strange woman, and frankly all I know about her is she gave birth to me sixteen years ago, and her husband was killed, and both sides of the family are a little better than trash. I don't know what she's going to expect from me. Money, love, regular visits, Mother's Day cards. It scares me, but I know I have to see her. And if Jamey's with me, we can talk about it on the trip back. He'll keep me from going crazy."

"He's real good at that," Kit said. "Ask Mother."

"I'm not Amanda," Val said. "I wish you'd try to understand."

"I understand," Kit replied. "I understand all sorts of things. I understand you didn't even think about me, about what I wanted. No, that isn't it. You didn't even remember I existed. You wanted your Jamey, you snapped your fingers, and Rick provided him for you. It was that simple. And why shouldn't it be? That's how your life's always been. You want something, you just ask Rick for it, and it's yours."

"That's not true," Val said. "I never wanted Mama to be sick, and there was nothing Daddy could do about that."

"But she was a Castaladi," Kit declared. "If only by marriage. It's the rest of the world you think you own, the way your father owns mine. The way you own me."

"I don't own you," Val said. "And Daddy certainly doesn't own Jamey." She looked away, at the wall where a painting once hung.

"I want you to leave," Kit said. "I'll be your employee's daughter, but I won't be your friend."

"That isn't fair," Val said. "Look, there's got to be a way out of this. I'll tell Daddy I don't want Jamey to come with me. I'll find someone else."

Kit remained silent.

"Terry," Val said. "I'll ask Terry to come instead. That's perfect. She's been a nervous wreck all week, and this way she'll know everything's okay between Daddy and her family. Sure she'll cry, but that's okay too. I bet I'll be crying. And with Bruno along, he'll know how to get us on the airplane and find us cabs and all that. Terry's just right. She was Mama's best friend, and she vowed to Mama she'd look after me. I'm sorry I ever thought of Jamey. Terry's much better, and that way you and Jamey can spend tomorrow together the way you wanted."

"What if Terry doesn't want to go?" Kit asked.

"She'll want to," Val replied. "If Daddy asks her, she'll want to."

Kit laughed. "It's that easy for you, isn't it," she said. "You're still just snapping your fingers."

"Maybe I am," Val said. "Maybe you're right about that. But I can't change overnight, Kit. At least give me the weekend to become a completely different person."

"My mother once told me that once you lose your innocence, you can't ever find it again," Kit said. "Change or don't change, Val. That's up to you. But don't think you'll find me where I was last week. I'm not there anymore, and I'm never going back."

Val stood up. "I can't go back either," she said. "So I

wouldn't have been looking for you there." She grabbed her books and her jacket. "Have a good weekend," she said. "I'll see myself out."

"Val," Kit said, but Val ignored her. Kit had one set of demons to deal with. Val had enough of her own.

Chapter 11

• • •

THE HOUSE, ON the outskirts of Buffalo, was small, maybe a quarter the size of the one Val grew up in. She tried to imagine what it had been like, with five young children elbowing for room, but it seemed overcrowded enough with just her, Bruno, Terry, and Carmela Primo inside it. The weather had turned ugly, and there was a raw wind that seemed to cut into the walls. The windows made a disconcerting, rattling sound.

"If you want, I'll lower the storms for you," Bruno offered.

"That'd be nice," Carmela replied. "Usually one of the boys does it, but the older they get, the less I can count on them."

"That's how it is with boys," Terry said. "I've got a batch of them myself."

Val looked around at the grownups and wished she had an army of contemporaries to protect her. Bruno began his self-appointed task.

"Would you like something to drink?" Carmela asked Terry. "Coffee maybe?"

Terry shook her head. "I'll just wait in the kitchen," she said. "You and Val can have your visit."

"Help yourself if you want something," Carmela said. "There's plenty of food in there."

"Thank you," Terry said.

Val sat down on a chair in the living room. Over the sofa was *The Last Supper*. Above the TV set was a painting of Jesus surrounded by little children. The furniture was covered with an orange-and-rust floral material, and the curtains were a green-and-brown plaid. She wished she could let Amanda loose on the room. Slashing could only improve it.

"You're a pretty girl," Carmela said. "You look like Charley, take after the Primo side."

Val nodded, as though she had always known that. She could see no resemblance between herself and Carmela, a heavy-set woman with graying hair and stubby, reddened hands. Her mother had had beautiful hands. She'd gone for manicures weekly before she got sick.

"I'd love a smoke," Carmela said.

"Go ahead," Val replied. "It won't bother me."

"I quit two years ago," Carmela declared. "The kids were after me to stop for years, and I finally did. My biggest accomplishment, quitting. But I'd sure love a cigarette now."

"Lots of people have trouble quitting," Val said. "Bob, that's Terry's husband, he must have tried quitting a dozen times. Daddy used to smoke, but he stopped when Mama got sick." She hadn't known whether she should say Daddy and Mama in front of Carmela, but she was too nervous to stop herself.

"It took me a couple of times too," Carmela said. "The kids, especially Marcie, were always leaving propaganda around the house. Things they'd get at school saying how bad smoking is for you. When they saw I wasn't reading it, they started reading it out loud to me. I'd be doing the dishes, and all of a sudden I'd hear this anti-smoking sermon. I quit when a friend of mine came down with lung cancer. I think it takes something like that to make you believe what cigarettes really do. My friend Marie. We went to school together, started smoking around the same time. I figured if it could happen to her, it could happen to me, so I quit. She died last winter."

"I'm sorry," Val said.

"Your mother died of cancer too, right?" Carmela replied. "What was it, lung?"

"I'm not sure," Val admitted. "Nobody ever really told me. She was sick for a very long time, I know that, and she had all kinds of treatments and surgery, but nothing seemed to work."

"That's a rough break," Carmela said. "Losing your mother when you're young like that. It was hard on my kids when their father died, and a father is nothing like a mother. At least Charley wasn't. It wasn't that he didn't love the kids. But he wasn't one for diapering or making Kool-Aid. I look at TV, and there are all these young fathers on, doing that sort of thing for their kids, and I try to picture Charley, and I just laugh. So how're your grades? You like that high school you go to?"

"It's fine," Val said. "I've been going there since kindergarten. My grades are all right."

"I always said Charley had a brain if he would only apply himself," Carmela declared. "But he wasn't a book kind of a person. Neither am I. I never read, except the magazines. I must read two or three magazines a month, plus the ones at the beauty parlor. I like the papers you can buy at the check-out lines. They're the only ones that tell you what's really happening with the stars. I pick them up sometimes. You like to read?"

"I read a lot when Mama was sick," Val replied. "We had to keep things pretty quiet, so reading was a good thing to do. I haven't done that much reading since then though. I guess I associate it with sickness."

"I've never been sick a day in my life," Carmela said. "Six times I gave birth, and all six times I was on my feet the next day. Of course with a lot of kids, you don't have time to get sick. Nobody's going to pamper you if you start sneezing. Charley didn't get sick much either. Sometimes his stomach would upset him a little, but I always thought that was nervousness. Charley could be a real nervous kind of a guy." She paused for a moment, then laughed. "Funny. I haven't talked this much about Charley in years. I haven't even thought about him this much. But ever since Rick called, well, it's natural I should think about Charley, and what things would have been like if he hadn't gotten himself killed like that. Sixteen years. I used to kid him about what an old man he was, he was a couple of years older than me, but now I can't believe he died so young. He was just thirty-one. He didn't like turning thirty at all, let me tell you. I gave him a big surprise party, and he damn near killed me. Not that he didn't love parties, or surprises for that matter. It was just turning thirty that got him down. His own father died when he was thirty-four, and Charley was always convinced he'd die at thirty-four too. He didn't make it even that long."

"How did his father die?" Val asked. Her grandfather.

"Car crash," Carmela replied. "Charley's mother was in the car too, and she was never much use after that. She died a couple of years after. It was natural Charley would run wild, his parents being like that. I come from a completely different type of family, the Rinaldis were much classier. My parents thought it was a big mistake, me marrying Charley, but I saw to it they had to agree. Charley Junior was born seven months to the day after Charley and I got married."

"Are your parents still alive?" Val asked.

Carmela shook her head. "Poppa died right after I got married," she said. "Heart attack. He was a young man too, younger than I am now. Mama died when I was pregnant with Marcie. The doctors never could figure out what was wrong with her. She was sick a long time, and had test after test, and the doctors would just shake their heads until finally she died. Marcie favors Mama, and I think it's because she was born so soon after Mama died. I wish she had a little more of Mama's personality though. I have five stubborn kids, and Marcie's the worst."

Six, Val thought. You have six stubborn kids.

"Sorry," Carmela said. "Leaving you out like that. Of course I don't know if you're stubborn or not. But if you take after Charley, you must be. The man was a mule. It's just . . . after I gave you away, I told everybody you died. The older kids knew different, but I didn't have much trouble convincing everybody else. I was crying all the time anyway, from missing Charley and being so scared, so they all thought I was crying because the baby died too. And my parents were dead, and so were Charley's, and suddenly Charley's brothers and sisters and my brothers and sisters were nowhere to be seen. I don't know how much Rick told you about Charley dying, but there was a mixup, and Charley was blamed for a lot of it. He might have even been to blame. Charley was a great one for playing the odds and ending up with a losing hand. Anyway, the Primos chose to forget Charley was a Primo, and the Rinaldis chose to forget I was a Rinaldi, and there I was with six young kids, and I wasn't even thirty, so I cried a lot. But I could never make myself tell people the truth about you. I guess I was too ashamed, that I'd actually let one of my babies go like that."

"Why did you?" Val asked. It wasn't an accusation, she was too grateful she'd been adopted to accuse. But she still had to know.

Carmela scratched her chin. "You cried a lot," she said. "No, that's the truth. Out of the six of them, you were the screamingest. Maybe you sensed what was going on. I always thought you were smart. You used to look at things different from the other kids. From the very first, I was afraid there was something wrong with you."

"Is that why?" Val asked. "You thought I wasn't good enough?"

"It wasn't a question of good. It was just different," Carmela said. "But if Charley had lived, nothing else would have happened. Maybe you wouldn't even have cried so much. It was just after he died, we had nothing, no money, and a mortgage on this house so big you could choke a horse, and kids gotta have food and shoes and heat in the winter. I didn't know what I was going to do. Usually in a situation like that, the widow's given some kind of settlement, but because of the mixup and everything, I figured I was lucky nobody was shooting at me. If Louie Castaladi hadn't shown up on my doorstep the way he did, I don't know what would have become of us."

"But you didn't want to give me up," Val said. "My father said you had to be persuaded."

Carmela laughed. "Louie Castaladi was a very persuasive man," she declared. "He had a lot of different ways of persuading."

"Did he threaten you?" Val asked.

"You sure you're not thirsty or something?" Carmela asked. "I bought soda for you. I don't drink much soda myself, and now with the kids all gone, I almost never have it in the house, so I bought three different kinds. I didn't know what you liked best."

"No, thank you," Val said. "Maybe later."

"I've only been on a plane once," Carmela said. "It sure made me thirsty."

"How did he persuade you?" Val asked.

Carmela laughed again. "You are Charley's daughter," she said. "He never let anything go. I remember once, I paid seventeen dollars for a dress and he thought it was way too much, I should've only paid ten, and he threw that in my face for years. I bet you're just like that, never forget a thing."

"Are you scared to tell me?" Val whispered. Maybe it was having Bruno, or even Terry, in the house that was keeping Carmela from admitting what actually had happened.

Carmela shook her head. "Not the way you think," she said. "You want to know the truth, fine, here's the truth. First I get some phone calls from people saying they represent Louie Castaladi. Now Louie is not exactly a stranger to me. He's godfather to our boy Vince. But we don't exactly travel in the same circles. So I start getting these phone calls, and the people say Louie's heard all about Charley, and what a shame it is, and me with six young kids, and the littlest one they hear is just a baby, a girl right? Like this makes a difference. So I'm crying, and the kids are screaming, and the baby's giving me these weird looks and refusing to nurse, like my milk's poison or something, and I don't know what the hell these guys are getting at. If Louie wants to give me some money, help out, fine. I'll take anything at that point. But they're not saying that. They're asking if the baby's okay. So I say sure. I mean, she was. She was strange maybe, but okay."

"You didn't suspect?" Val asked.

"Why should I?" Carmela asked. "Nobody's been calling me over the years saying Barbara Castaladi can't have kids. Not that it surprises me once I learn. My mother's cousin married into that family, and all you ever heard about them was how sick they all were. Anyway, I keep thanking these representatives of Louie Castaladi for their phone calls, and nothing really seems to be getting said. Then one evening, the doorbell rings, and there's Louie himself. Looking very handsome. And he strolls in like he's always in this part of Buffalo, it's practically his second home, and his bodyguard hands me a bag of groceries that Louie says he just picked up in case I need anything. I don't even have food for breakfast the next day, and there's milk and bacon and eggs all in this bag. So I start crying. I think Louie's come to save me. Now we won't starve. Now the welfare people won't start sniffing at my heels. Now I won't have to pick which kids should end up in foster care, which kids can I keep. Louie Castaladi has arrived with groceries. It's all going to be all right."

"You were thinking about foster care?" Val asked.

"I have six kids, no money," Carmela replied. "Charley Junior is twelve, already he's getting into trouble. I was thinking maybe if I put two, even three, kids into foster care, I'll be able to take care of the rest. It wasn't what I wanted. I hated the idea of my kids being shuffled around like that. But nobody was offering me a lot of choices."

Val looked around the living room. She could hear Bruno and Terry in the kitchen. Bruno must have finished with the storm windows, and she hadn't even noticed. All these kids Carmela was talking about, Charley Junior and Marcie and Vince, were her brothers and sisters. She didn't know any of them, and yet she could imagine their pain at being torn away from their home, their mother, to go to live with strangers.

"So Louie sits down," Carmela said. "The kids take one look at him, at his bodyguard, they all run to their rooms. The baby, for a change, is not screaming. I'm crying, but it's more from gratitude than anything else. Louie Castaladi remembers our connection. He remembers Charley is part Castaladi, they share blood. He's our savior. I would have kissed his ring if he'd asked me."

"But he asked for the baby instead," Val said.

Carmela nodded. "He starts out with a lot of questions," she declared. "How am I doing, do we have enough. We don't, so I tell him so. He asks after the health of all the kids. He even remembers their names. Finally he comes to the baby, says he loves babies, would I mind if he had a look at her. I'm not going to turn this man down anything, so we go to the girls' room, and there you are, looking so peaceful and innocent, it had to be an act. Only Louie doesn't know this. He thinks you're always like this. 'An angel,' he says, and I don't say otherwise. Maybe if he thinks you're an angel, he'll bring us more groceries next week. So we go back downstairs, and he offers me some sympathy. How rough it must be, losing Charley that way, especially with all the misunderstandings going on, and he's talked to the head of the Petrollis to see what can be done, only they spit at the name of Charley Primo. So he doesn't think I can look for help from them. And I open my heart to him, tell him how the Primos and the Rinaldis all have forgotten I even exist, and what am I going to do, six kids to feed, and a mortgage to pay off, and Louie's sitting there listening and nodding his head like this is the worst problem he's ever heard, and it's going to take a lot of thinking for him to come up with an answer, but he's going to try if it kills him. I even stop crying. The kids are quiet for the first time in their lives, and there's a kind of a peace all around, and Louie is nodding."

Terry laughed suddenly in the kitchen. Both Val and Carmela stopped for a moment, startled by the sound. "She's a nice woman," Carmela said. "Coming all this way to be with you."

"She was my mother's best friend," Val said. "She made a vow to look after me, when my mother was dying."

"That's good," Carmela said. "To have people who love you. You're a lucky girl."

"I know," Val said. "I really do."

"It all worked out then," Carmela said.

Val nodded. "I know that," she said. "But I need to know how."

"Just like Charley and that dress," Carmela said. "All right. Louie's being Mr. Sympathy, and I'm eating it up. And then like he's just had this thought, he says to me have I thought about giving the baby up for adoption? So I say no. I guess I scream it, and it's a miracle the baby doesn't wake up and start screaming the way she always did. I mean foster care is bad enough, but at least you can get the kids back when you can afford them, sort of like a pawnshop. Adoption, the kid's gone forever. I'm never doing that to any of my own. Which I tell him, in no uncertain terms. And Louie's nodding again, like he's really listening, but then he says what if the baby goes to a home so wonderful, so perfect, it's got to be the best thing that ever happened to her. And I still say no, not one of mine, I could never do that to one of mine. And Louie's looking at me really intently now, and he says what if the baby's brought up by family, not by strangers you have no control over, but by blood. So I ask him what blood. I'm still not sure just what's going on, but all of a sudden, I'm beginning to worry the baby's going to start screaming, and Louie'll leave."

"I screamed that much?" Val asked.

"All the time," Carmela replied. "You only stopped screaming when you'd want to give me one of those funny looks of yours. And I started thinking about that then, about what a funny baby you were, and you never seemed to warm up to me the way all my other babies had, and how you wouldn't nurse unless I practically forced you. And Louie's offering me blood. So I figure I'd better hear him out. And he says his son Ricky, fine boy, in business for himself, construction, strictly legitimate, married for years to a lovely girl, Barbara Salvati, but they can't have kids, and they've been to all the doctors, and it's breaking their hearts. And here I am with six healthy children, the youngest an angel, and all Barbara wants is just one baby to call her own, and Charley is part Castaladi after all, so even though I don't know Rick and Barbara, it isn't like I'd be handing the baby over to a stranger. And I start getting mad."

"Why?" Val asked, half-convinced herself that Carmela should give the baby away on the spot.

"I'm not going to sell no baby of mine for a bag of groceries and a little sympathy," Carmela declared. "Not with five others to feed and a mortgage to pay. And I tell him that. I tell Louie Castaladi, who owns all of Jersey and half of New York, that no matter how fine his son Ricky might be, and no matter how sad Barbara is, my children do not come cheap. And Louie agrees. He snaps his fingers and his bodyguard shows up with a briefcase, which Louie opens. He takes out an envelope, hands it over to me, and inside is ten thousand dollars. And suddenly I'm scared, because I've never seen that kind of money before in my life, and it'll buy a lot of bacon and eggs for the kids."

"You sold me?" Val asked.

"I did what I had to," Carmela said. "I thought about the other five kids, the ones I really knew, and what ten thousand could do for them. Keep them out of foster care for one thing. But I still had some pride. I am a Rinaldi, after all, so I said to Louie ten thousand was nice, but I needed a lot more than that, and he says how much, and I realize I have him. He'll give me anything so his son's wife can have a baby for her own. And I say I'm giving up my own baby, the last child I could ever have with Charley, and how do I know she'll be all right? Louie says he's giving me his word and isn't that enough, and I say usually yes, but in this case he should understand I need more. So Louie asks how about if we stay in touch. He'll make sure Rick understands and he'll send me pictures so I can see you growing up, and I can let him know if the baby's brothers and sisters ever need for anything. Which I take to be a pretty generous offer. It's like you'd be supporting them, which was more than I could do, or Charley Junior, him being only twelve. And I'm thinking I'd better say yes fast before the baby starts squalling, so I shake Louie's hand and he snaps his fingers again, and there's the bodyguard with everything you need to move a baby. And Louie himself goes upstairs, and takes the baby out of her crib, and tells me I'll never be sorry, and I'm crying, and the other kids are up now, asking what's going on, but the baby keeps sleeping, which I regard as a sign from God that I'm doing the right thing, and Louie and the bodyguard leave the house and leave Buffalo, and that's the last I see of you until an hour ago today. Except for pictures. So now you know everything, just the way you wanted, and I hope you're satisfied because these haven't been easy memories for me, and it's a story I don't want to have to tell again."

Val nodded. She was too stunned to cry, and then she felt like a fool for being so startled. Of course money had changed hands. That was how Rick Castaladi did things, on a cash basis.

Carmela Primo looked at her daughter. "You turned out real pretty," she said. "You look more like Vince than any of the others. I guess now you want to see some pictures? I pulled them out when I heard you were coming. I didn't tell the boys, or Marcie for that matter, about you. Most of them think you died anyway."

"Yes," Val said. "Pictures would be nice."

Carmela opened up a shoe-box. "I keep meaning to buy a nice album, put the pictures in," she said. "Here's Marcie when she graduated high school. And this one is of Charley Junior and Donny playing football. Vince took that picture. I got him a camera one year, and he took some pictures then. Here's Marcie again, at her tenth birthday. Oh, and here's Vince. I guess he gave up the camera long enough for someone to take a picture of him. See, he really does look like you."

Val handled the picture gingerly. It was slightly out of focus, but even so she could see a boy who looked enough like her to be her brother. "What's he like?" she asked. "Vince, I mean."

Carmela shrugged. "He's been in a little trouble," she said. "All the boys have. But I think he's straightening himself out. Here's Charley Junior on his wedding day. He and Jennifer have two kids, a boy and a girl."

"I'm an aunt?" Val asked.

Carmela laughed. "I guess so," she said. "Donny's wife Diane's expecting too. The baby's due in March. If you want, you could come up for the baptism."

"I don't know," Val said. "I guess it'll depend on what's happening at school."

Carmela leafed through the pictures. "Here's the one I've been looking for," she said. "That was a proud moment for me, when one of mine actually graduated college. She was already a member of the order, that's why she's not wearing a cap and gown. But it's her college graduation picture all right."

She handed the picture over to Val. This one was in focus. Standing proud and tall, clutching her diploma, was Sister Gina Marie.

Chapter 12

• • •

VAL TIMED IT so she arrived at school right before the bell rang on Monday. She wasn't prepared to talk to Kit or Michelle, and had avoided their phone calls the day before by telling Connie to say she had a headache. She'd used the same lie fairly effectively with her father. It didn't matter whether any of them believed her. It was simply a signal of her need to be left alone.

Kit was absent again, and Michelle, with a sensitivity Val had never credited her with, kept away as well. Val knew Terry must have described at least part of Saturday to her, the flight to Buffalo, the teary flight back. She wasn't sure how much of her conversation with Carmela Terry had overhead, and how much of that Terry would tell her daughter. She didn't much care, right then, just as long as she wasn't plagued by questions.

The morning took forever. Val's teachers, unaware that her entire life had turned and overturned and overturned again in the course of a week, persisted in treating her as though she were a student. Val tried to marshal her talent for concentration, but her mind kept drifting back to a hundred different images. Carmela's hideous living room. Shannon O'Roarke. Kit in her robe and pajamas. The demolished kitchen. Her father's face when she told him that she knew. Her mother lying in bed, listening to Val's school stories. Sister Gina Marie's photograph.

Twice she was called on, and twice she didn't know the answer, or even what the question had been, and twice she was reprimanded. It didn't seem to matter. Nothing mattered anymore, at least not schoolwork.

Eventually it was lunchtime, and Val knew what she had to do. She walked to Sister Gina Marie's classroom, and found her sitting at her desk, grading papers.

"May I come in?" Val asked from the doorway.

Sister Gina Marie looked up and smiled at her. "I've been expecting you," she said. "Come on in, and close the door behind you if you want."

"Thank you," Val said. She walked to the front of the class and sat at the desk Kit used. Kit was small and always sat in the first row.

Sister Gina Marie pushed the papers away. "Sometimes I skip lunch to catch up with my paperwork," she said. "No matter how I try to schedule myself, I always seem to be behind."

Val nodded, although her father had brought her up to respect deadlines and always meet them.

"Mama called me," Sister Gina Marie said. "First on Friday, and then Saturday evening. So I have some idea of what went on."

"That's good," Val said. "Because I'm hopelessly confused."

Sister Gina Marie laughed. "You have had a week of it," she said. "It'll take you a while to adjust."

"I don't even know what I'm supposed to adjust to," Val said. "I talked to a couple of people last week about being adopted, and they both grew up knowing they were adopted, and they've never met their natural parents. In one week, not only did I find out, but I met her. My mother I mean, and now I have brothers and sisters, and a family history, no, not just one family history, at least two, the Primos and the Castaladis, not to mention all those sickly Salvatis and classy Rinaldis, and I used to know exactly who I was and what I was supposed to do and who I was supposed to become, and now I don't know anything." Val pounded the desk with her fist. "You know something? It really isn't fair."

Sister Gina Marie smiled. "It isn't all bad," she said. "Sometimes it's good to get shaken up. It makes all the pieces fit together in a different pattern."

"Like what?" Val asked. "I had a father who loved me. Well, I still do, but he isn't my father anymore. Not biologically at least. I'm a distant cousin. We share just enough blood for him to take me into his house. He loves me, I know he loves me, but he brought me up to believe I had to be obedient. Obedient and respectful. I should obey him and Mama and the sisters and the priests and Bruno and Connie and my aunts and uncles, and now I don't want to obey any of them, starting with Daddy. He doesn't obey the law, so why should I obey him?"

"Do you know he doesn't obey the law?" Sister Gina Marie asked. "Or are you just assuming that because you're so angry?"

"That's one of the things I'm angry about," Val said. "All these years of pretending Rick Castaladi is a respectable businessman. I don't think he kills people, but there are other ways of breaking the law. And I don't see why I have to accept that just because he gave me a home and love and rules to live by. I hate his rules. I hate him."

"Is there anyone you don't hate right now?" Sister Gina Marie asked.

Val shook her head. "I hate the whole rotten stinking world," she replied.

"Good," Sister Gina Marie said. "Because that won't last. Sooner or later, you'll start liking someone again, and then someone else, and before you know it, you'll forget about hating the whole rotten stinking world."

"How would you know?" Val asked. "You're a nun. You're not allowed to hate."

"I wasn't always a nun," Sister Gina Marie replied. "There was a long time when I hated the world too."

"When?" Val asked.

Sister Gina Marie gazed out the window. The weather had turned warm, and the sunlight poured in. "When Poppa died," she replied. "I hated the world for a long time after that."

"I didn't hate the world when my mother died," Val said. "I was more relieved than anything else."

"Different kinds of death," Sister Gina Marie said. "Poppa left the house right after breakfast one morning, and was dead before lunchtime. They called us at school to tell us. Charley Junior and Donny went to Holy Cross, and I went to St. Elizabeth's, so we were told separately. Vince was in kindergarten that year, but they didn't tell him. He came home to find out. I remember because Mama was crying, she was just hysterical, and Vince didn't know what was going on, so I had to tell him, and that made me even angrier. I was the second oldest in the family, but I was the oldest girl, and that meant I had a lot of the child-rearing responsibilities. Mama couldn't handle us all, even when Poppa was alive. So I had to tell Vince that Poppa had died and gone to heaven, which I had my doubts about, and he was crying, and then Marcie, who didn't understand what was going on, started crying too, and that got the baby going, and it felt like I was the only one who wasn't crying, so I was the one who had to wipe the tears and pull everyone together. I hated Mama so much that moment. I hated her more later, but I wouldn't have believed that if you'd told me. I wouldn't have believed there could be more hate than what I felt just then."

"Your mother said I cried a lot," Val said. "My mother. I don't even have a vocabulary for all these people."

"Why don't you call her Carmela?" Sister Gina Marie suggested. "It won't bother me."

"Thank you," Val said. "What do I call you?"

"I like Sister," Sister Gina Marie replied. "It has so many meanings."

Val smiled.

"You cried all the time," Sister Gina Marie declared. "I suppose you were just colicky at first, and then you sensed all the tension. That day when Poppa died, the funny thing was, neither Charley Junior or I really knew what it meant. Donny was the one who figured it all out. Donny's very smart, maybe the smartest of all of us. He was only eight, but he grabbed Charley and me and explained just what was going on. That Poppa was accused of setting the shooting up, but had gotten it in the crossfire anyway. That the name of Primo was mud. He actually said that, and I knew he was right, and it left me feeling ashamed to be a Primo, which was why I've never used it, at least not in the classroom. Charley got all cocky and defensive about it, so he's Charley Primo Junior to anyone and everyone. He could drop the Junior at this point, Poppa's been dead for sixteen years now, but he won't. We all dealt with the dishonor different ways."

"It must have been horrible," Val said.

"It was worse than you can imagine," Sister Gina Marie replied. "No one came to the funeral. Poppa came from a large family, and so did Mama, and it was as though we'd never existed. Even the priest was in a hurry to get us out of there. Mama was screaming and carrying on. She has a real operatic streak, and I can't blame her for being upset, losing her husband when she was so young, and having six kids to raise, but she didn't think about what she was doing to the little ones. Vince has never been the same. He was such an outgoing little boy, really sweet, and after the funeral, he became withdrawn, then surly. Marcie, who was born stubborn, became an absolute mule. Donny wet his bed every night for weeks, which Mama regarded as an act of disobedience, so she'd smack him for it, and wish Poppa were alive to give him a real whipping. You can imagine what that did to Donny."

"No," Val said. "I can't."

"Nothing good," Sister Gina Marie said. "Meanwhile, Charley Junior is getting into fights every day at school, and within a week of Poppa's death, Mama's realizing she has no money. Nothing. They were never ones for saving anyway, and with six kids there were a lot of expenses. They were still paying off the medical bills from the baby. Mama had some friends left, and they'd come over and talk about what was to become of us. Mama had never had a job in her life. She hadn't even graduated high school. Charley Junior and I were too young to work." Sister Gina Marie took a deep breath. "She was only a couple of years older than I am," she said. "I forget that sometimes, because she always seemed so old to me. But she wasn't even thirty, and her life was over. When I get angry at her, and I still do, I have to remember that."

"She mentioned to me that she thought about putting some of you in foster care," Val said. "That she didn't want to."

Sister Gina Marie laughed. "I'm not sure about that didn't want to part," she said. "Every day she threatened a different one of us with it. Except me. She knew she needed me. The problem was picking and choosing. Charley Junior was getting into all those fights, but he was her first born, and he carried Poppa's name. Donny was a real possibility, but in a lot of ways Mama depended on him, because he was so smart, and he could figure out the angles. Vince was Mama's favorite, so she really didn't want to part with him. That left Marcie and the baby. Marcie was two, and Mama suspected if she put her or the baby in foster care, there'd be a lot of pressure put on her to relinquish rights, let the girls be adopted. In addition, Marcie was my favorite, and Mama knew there'd be real trouble with me if Marcie was boarded out. And I was the one changing the diapers and washing the sheets and making a jar of peanut butter last for two weeks. So she wasn't about to alienate me."

"No wonder you were so angry," Val said.

Sister Gina Marie laughed. "It got worse," she said. "Because right around the time we were reaching bottom, Mama started getting phone calls from representatives of Louie Castaladi. Mama thought we kids didn't know about them, but of course we did. Donny had a real gift for eavesdropping and putting two and two together. And Mama was looking at the baby differently, with less resentment and anger. She used to pick the baby up and shake her to make her stop crying, and she stopped doing that. She caught Vince once teasing the baby, and she slapped him really hard. She never hit Vince. And then one night a limo drove up, and there was Louie Castaladi himself, and Mama ran to me and said 'give the baby some wine, she's got to stay asleep,' so I did. Two hours later, you were out of there, still sleeping. I bet you had an awful hangover when you woke up."

"So she knew," Val said. "She thought of me as a commodity too."

"She was desperate," Sister Gina Marie replied. "And she really wanted what was best for her children. Now I can find it in my heart to forgive her. Then I just hated her, not for selling one of her children, I knew how much we needed that money, but for seeming to be so casual about it. She cried that night, but she never cried again, at least not where I could hear her. And she made all of us lie and say the baby had died, which I was sure was a jinx and the baby would die as a result. I was always relieved when Rick sent us pictures, and I could see you were still alive."

"But you stopped hating," Val said. "How could you?"

Sister Gina Marie laughed. "Hating takes a lot of energy," she said. "And I was still raising Donny and Vince and Marcie. Not to mention going to school and looking out for Charley Junior, and Mama for that matter. Time passed, and I began to forget what the baby looked like, how tiny and sweet she'd been. I put all my energies into Marcie. I was determined she'd escape from us all. And I succeeded. She went to boarding school on full scholarship and now she's at Marymount. I think you'll like her."

"Do I have to meet her?" Val asked.

"That's entirely up to you," Sister Gina Marie replied.

"I've been an only child all my life," Val said. "And now I have all these brothers and sisters, and they're not little kids any more. They have kids of their own. And I don't know if I'll like any of them, but they all terrify me. And I don't think Daddy would much like me to get close to them. We haven't talked about it, because we haven't talked about anything, but knowing Daddy, he'd see it as a betrayal. Which it might be. I threw up three times yesterday, and all I could remember was how Carmela said Charley had an upset stomach. I mean, is that my inheritance from him? A weak stomach?"

"You look like him," Sister Gina Marie replied. "You and Vince both."

"Carmela showed me a couple of pictures," Val said. "Of Charley. And no insult intended, but all he looked like was a hood."

"That's what he was," Sister Gina Marie replied. "A small-time hood."

"That is great," Val said. "My heredity is small-time hood. My environment is big-time hood. I guess that makes me a mid-sized model."

"It makes you whoever you want to be," Sister Gina Marie declared. "My father was a hood and my mother a hysteric, and I became a nun and a teacher."

"I don't want to be a nun either," Val said.

"Neither does Marcie," Sister Gina Marie replied. "Callings aren't genetic."

Val hesitated. "I have a couple of questions I really want to ask you," she said. "Personal ones. May I?"

Sister Gina Marie nodded.

"Are you here because of me?" Val asked. "Did you know I was a student here when you began to teach?"

"I knew," Sister Gina Marie replied. "I didn't become a teacher just to run into you, but I knew where you were. Rick's always been good about keeping Mama informed. And when I graduated with my teaching degree and was told there was an opening here, I asked for it. I was lucky. Most of the other sisters who graduated at the same time were dedicated to eradicating poverty and asked for inner-city schools. So they needed someone to teach the daughters of the wealthy."

"So it's no coincidence that you're here," Val said.

"None," Sister Gina Marie replied. "It worked out very well, actually. I like it here a lot. And I get to give Mama reports occasionally about how you're doing. She loves to hear about you."

Val wasn't sure she cared to know that. "I still have one more question," she said. "I don't know why it's so important to me, but it is."

"Ask," Sister Gina Marie said.

"Did you become a nun because of who your parents were?" Val asked. "Is it some form of penance for what they did?"

"Oh, no," Sister Gina Marie said. "I pray for them, for the salvation of their souls, but that's all I can do. I haven't sacrificed my life for them, if that's what you mean."

"Would you have become a nun no matter what?" Val asked. "Even if you'd had parents like Caroline O'Mara's?"

"The night that Louie Castaladi took the baby, I prayed for her," Sister Gina Marie said. "I'd always prayed in school and at church of course, but this was different. I prayed for the baby the next night too, and the night after that. Then I found myself praying for Poppa's immortal soul, and every night before going to sleep, I prayed for the two of you. And those prayers comforted me. I started thinking about Marcie next, how much I wanted for her, and I began to include her in my prayers. Vince was next, then Donny, and finally even Charley Junior and Mama. And I didn't just pray in my bedroom either. I'd stop in at church on my way home from school, and I'd light a candle and pray. After a while, I didn't pray for individuals anymore. It was more than that. And I realized the only time I felt complete was when I was praying. Not just at peace. Any time away from the house was bound to offer me some peace. It was more a sense of wholeness, of being where I belonged. I spoke to Sister Bernadette about it when I was sixteen. She was my history teacher, and I really loved her. She said she wasn't surprised, and I knew then where I belonged."

"I wish I knew," Val said. "I used to."

"You will again," Sister Gina Marie said.

Val shook her head. "I tried praying," she said. "I went to church yesterday for Mass. Connie likes to go, so I went with her. But it just felt like more lies."

"That may change," Sister Gina Marie said.

"Here's the problem," Val declared. "A week ago my mother was dead, but I knew who she was. She loved me, and we used to run away to the movies together. And my father was great. He spent time with me, and when he had to be away on business he always called, and I respected him and loved him. Now I find out my mother was someone so frightened of my father, or so brainwashed, she didn't even ask where the baby she was told to raise came from. And my father is a man who buys everything he wants—politicians, babies, the loyalty of friends. And I have two new parents to deal with too, a father who not only was a small-time hood, but a disloyal one, and a mother who for whatever reasons sold me, and I don't think she ever really loved me. How am I supposed to be any sort of person coming from all that? You had prayer, you had a special relationship with God. I have nothing."

"You have more than nothing," Sister Gina Marie said.

"I'm not faulting you for seeing it that way right now, but you really do have a lot."

"Oh, I know that," Val said. "I have pretty clothes and a lavender bedroom and a father who'll probably give me anything just so I'll keep loving him. How could I forget? I have my own bodyguard. I'm the luckiest girl in the world."

"You're a lot luckier than you think you are," Sister Gina Marie declared. "You have four parents who love you. Some people don't even have one."

"Four?" Val asked. "That's at least three more than I can count."

"Four," Sister Gina Marie replied. "Starting with Poppa, our father. I remember the day he carried you home from the hospital. He was so delighted with you. Even then it was obvious you looked like him. He danced around the living room with you, called you his princess. It's funny. At the time he just made me mad, because Marcie got jealous, and I was the one who had to comfort her. But now I find it a very joyous memory, how Poppa danced around the living room with you. He was dead within the month, and I don't think he was ever that happy again."

Val tried to picture the man she'd met only through snapshots dancing around with her and calling her princess. But the snapshots were faded and refused to come to life.

"Mama loved you too," Sister Gina Marie said. "Not very well, I grant you, but she loved you. She loved all her babies. She still loves us, and believe me, we're not an easy bunch to love. And maybe she stopped crying when Rick adopted you because she knew she'd done what was best for you. I don't think you doubt that, that everything worked out for the best."

"No," Val said. "I know that."

Sister Gina Marie nodded. "Your mother must have

loved you," she said. "That's obvious in a thousand different ways. You're not angry at her, for one thing, even though she was a part of this lie. And there's a gentleness when you speak about her that isn't there any other time."

"And Daddy?" Val asked.

"You know how much he loves you," Sister Gina Marie said. "No matter how angry you are, you know that."

"So where does that leave me?" Val asked. "If all these people are saints and I love them, do I have to be like them?"

"You take what's best from them," Sister Gina Marie said. "And you hold onto that and cherish it. The parts you don't like or can't respect, you reject. That's what I've done, and it's worked pretty well for me."

"It sounds too easy," Val said.

"We both know better," Sister Gina Marie said. "But if I can do it, I know you can."

Val nodded. Her lunch period was about over, and she still had a long day ahead of her. "Do we have to tell people?" she asked. "That we're sisters, I mean. Would it offend you if we didn't?"

"That's up to you," Sister Gina Marie said. "I'll accept whatever you decide."

Val smiled. Sister Gina Marie was a trusty. It was good to have one in her corner.

The bell rang, and Val knew she would have to leave. "I keep forgetting to ask," she said. "What was my name? When I was a baby."

"Lauren," Sister Gina Marie said. "Lauren Michelle. Mama heard it on one of her soap operas, and she thought it was pretty."

Lauren, Val thought. A perfectly nice name. But it wasn't hers.

Chapter 13

• • •

As BRUNO DROVE into the driveway, Val spotted Kit standing by the evergreens. "Leave me out here," she said, so Bruno stopped the car long enough for Val to get out. Val walked over to Kit, suddenly feeling shy. After sixteen years of friendship, she was no longer sure she really knew Kit. Then again, after sixteen years of living, she was no longer sure she knew herself either. Kit was just part of the chaos.

"Hi," Val said. "Are you all right?"

"I'm not sick, if that's what you mean," Kit said. "Sorry. Everything that comes out of my mouth these days sounds angry."

Val laughed. "Everything out of mine sounds crazy," she said.

Kit nodded. "I wanted to talk with you. I guess I felt I owed it to you to talk. Only I couldn't do it at school, and I wasn't ready to yesterday. I thought I was, so I called, but Connie said you had a headache, and I was so relieved I didn't have to talk with you it was scary."

"I wasn't ready either," Val said. "That's why I had Connie tell people I had a headache."

"How was school?" Kit asked. "I was kind of surprised you went."

"It was better than being home," Val replied. "Do you want to come in?"

"No," Kit said. "Let's talk here, okay?"

"Okay," Val said. She put her books on the damp ground. Let them rot, she thought, and the savagery of the image cheered her immediately.

"I hated being angry at you," Kit said.

"I hated having you angry," Val said.

"The thing is," Kit said, "I still am. Angry I mean. And I'm not sure I'm going to stop being angry, even though I want to."

"How much of it is angry at me?" Val asked. "And how much is angry at everything?"

"I haven't worked out the percentages yet," Kit said, and for the first time in days, she sounded like Kit. "This is very hard."

"I think that's what we're majoring in," Val said. "Very Hard."

"I'm ready for a postgraduate degree," Kit replied. "Val, you're my best friend. I've always loved you and looked up to you and envied you. Even when your mother was sick, I envied you. My mother was just as sick, and she wasn't going to die, even if I wanted her to. I used to hate myself, being jealous of someone whose mother was dying, but I was. The day of her funeral, Mother didn't want to go, and Pop made her, physically made her, and when it was over, we came back home, and Mother got as drunk as I've ever seen her, and she threw up all over the living room. I don't know why she bothered. Pop wasn't around, he'd gone to your house to be with Rick, and Kevin was away at school, so that just left me, and all I did was clean up. It wasn't like I'd love her more because she threw up. Not if I had to clean it. And I was so jealous of you it cut into my heart. You were home surrounded by all those Castaladis, and you had your father and mine too for that matter, and all I had was that mess, which I couldn't let Pop see. I remembered that yesterday, the way you remembered Shannon O'Roarke. Things that are important, only you can't make yourself realize it at the time."

"I'm sorry about your mother," Val said. "You should see mine."

"Was she awful?" Kit asked. "I wanted her to be awful."

"She wasn't great," Val replied. "Basically she sold me to the Castaladis. She didn't care what sort of people were going to bring me up, just as long as they paid cash and kept on paying it."

"I wish someone had bought me," Kit declared. "That isn't really it. I wish your family had bought me. Not the way they've bought Pop. I wish they'd thought of me instead of you, and I could have been Val Castaladi."

Val laughed. "I'm sorry," she said. "But Daddy never would have taken in an Irish kid."

"I still wish I could have been Val Castaladi," Kit said.

"There are times when I wished I was you," Val replied. "Times with your mother that I never had with mine. There's a way Amanda has of looking at things, cutting through the crap, that I always thought was magic. And I loved how Jamey respected you. He didn't just expect it from you, the kind of blind obedience Daddy trained me to have, but he actually respected you, listened to what you had to say."

"Pop has to respect me," Kit declared. "I'm the one who cleans up all the messes. His as well as Mother's. Respect is what he gives me because he counts on me so much."

"I've counted on you too," Val said. "Always. Can I still do that, Kit? Can I still count on you?"

"I don't think so," Kit said.

Val felt a pain as intense as any she'd suffered during the past week. "Why?" she asked. "Just because of Saturday?"

"How honest do you want me to be?" Kit asked.

"I don't know," Val said. "Start at completely, and if I can't handle it, I'll tell you."

"All right," Kit said. "I don't come off real good in this version."

"Nobody has," Val replied. "Not recently."

A flock of birds flew overhead in a V-shape. "It must be nice to do that," Kit said. "Change your life every six months."

"They're always birds," Val said. "That doesn't change."

"I'd still like to give it a try," Kit declared. "All right. The truth. The truth is Mother never wanted us to be friends. She never wanted me to go to Most Precious Blood. It was bad enough as far as she was concerned that I was Catholic, I didn't have to be brought up as one. Only Pop insisted. Do you remember, when we were little, Mother never brought me over to your house. It was always Pop. She wasn't even drinking then, not much at any rate, but she never went to your house. She wouldn't let Kevin anywhere near it. Rick wanted to go to a baseball game once with Pop and Kevin, and Mother forbade it. She told Pop she'd leave him and she'd take Kevin with her and he'd never find them again if he let Rick anywhere near Kevin. Part of me didn't understand that, but most of me was jealous that she loved Kevin enough to protect him. Maybe she felt I was already lost, or maybe she just didn't care that much about me."

"Amanda hates us that much?" Val asked. "I never thought she hated me."

"Mother hates everybody," Kit replied. "Except maybe for Kevin. She and Pop negotiated. Made quid pro quo agreements. Mother would be nice to you, civil to Rick and Barbara. In exchange for which none of the other Castaladis would ever be invited to our house, and Kevin would be sent to prep school. I called Kevin at school yesterday, to ask him how it was he got sent off to school when he was twelve, and he told me that was the deal. He begged to go before then, but Pop wouldn't let him. That's one of the things he hates Pop for, making him stay at home. There are lots of other things too, of course. Kevin's a first-class hater. He takes after Mother that way."

"Like what?" Val asked. "What other things?"

Kit shrugged. "Nothing big," she said. "It doesn't take big things if you're primed for hating. You want an example? When Kevin was at school, I guess he was sixteen, Pop got tickets for a Giants game. Three tickets on the fifty-yard line. He offered them as a bribe to Kevin to get him to come home for a weekend. He told him to bring a friend, but by that point Kevin wasn't bringing anyone home, so Pop said he'd take Kevin and me instead. Only he mentioned the tickets to Rick, who said he wanted them, so naturally Pop let Rick have them. And Kevin didn't come home. He skipped Thanksgiving too that year, and he was threatening to miss Christmas too, only I called him up and begged him. Mother was in awful shape, and I was afraid she'd kill herself if Kevin didn't show up for Christmas. He stayed two days, and all he did was scream at Pop about the damn football game. I mean it was nothing. I didn't mind giving you the tickets, but to

Kevin it was a mortal sin. No, that isn't right. It was a convenient symbol of everything Pop had given up for Rick. Kevin's always been fond of convenient symbols, like boycotting home for the holidays."

Val remembered the game, the perfection of the day, the silver fox coat. "I'm sorry," she said. "I wish you'd gone instead of us."

"One game wouldn't have made any difference," Kit replied. "It just gave Kevin something else to be angry about. Kevin likes being angry. He likes it more than Mother does. That's why he doesn't drink."

Val rested her back against one of the evergreens. "You must have been angry too," she said. "Not just because of the football game. Because of everything."

Kit shook her head. "I was more jealous than anything else," she replied. "Jealous because you had a big wonderful family of cousins and aunts and uncles, and Mother wouldn't let me near them. I used to picture you and Michelle together playing with dolls while I'd be home alone reading. I didn't even like dolls and I never much liked Michelle and I was jealous anyway. Then at school the other kids' mothers wouldn't let me play with them. You never seemed to mind that, I guess because you had so much family, but it bothered me a lot."

"You should have told Daddy," Val said. "Maybe he could have done something."

Kit laughed. "What?" she said. "Gotten half the school transferred to Detroit? It was okay after a while. I figured things out pretty fast. If I was nice to everybody, then everybody would be nice back to me. So what if they weren't my friends. You were, and I didn't need anything more than that. Only I couldn't risk losing you, so I did whatever you wanted, and after a while, I got to thinking it was your due, sort of the way Pop feels about Rick. It was right that everybody loved you and kissed you and acted as though you were special. You were special, and I was lucky that you let me be your friend."

"But you were special too," Val said. "You were always the smartest girl in our class. You've always done best in school."

"I didn't have any choice," Kit said. "I flunked a test once, in sixth grade, just to see what would happen. Pop had to sign it, Mother was too drunk to, and he looked straight at me and said he would have been nothing, nothing, without his brains, and the only chance I had in life was if I applied myself a hundred percent all the time and got the grades I was capable of. So I did. There was a year I used to punish myself for every point under a hundred I got on any of my tests. Don't ask me how. It was pretty gross."

"I wish you'd told me," Val said.

"Why?" Kit asked. "What could you have done? Besides, your mother was sick. You cried a lot that year. I didn't want to make things worse for you."

"You still should have told me," Val said. "We were friends. I would have listened."

"I know that," Kit said. "I knew it then. I knew you loved me. You were a trusty. You saw Mother drunk, and you loved me anyway. Up until this week, I would have killed for you, the same as Pop would do for Rick."

"What happened this week?" Val asked.

"I found out you weren't a Castaladi," Kit declared. "Dumb, isn't it? But all of a sudden I thought why am I doing all this for her? Why am I protecting her and defending her and helping her with her schoolwork and wiping away her tears when she isn't special at all? She's as much a nothing as I am. And I didn't have any answers. Hell, there's no trick to being adopted. Anyone can be adopted."

"You're wrong," Val said. "There are plenty of tricks to being adopted."

"Maybe I'm wrong about everything," Kit said. "But Thursday Malcolm came over because he knew I needed him, and you must have known how much I needed him, but you whisked him away from me anyway, just because you were too impatient to wait for Bruno to get off the phone. That never would have bothered me before, because you were Val Castaladi, and that was your right. Only on Thursday, you weren't Val Castaladi anymore, you were just some stranger leading Val Castaladi's life, and you lost your right to take what you wanted from me. I didn't know it then, but I had started to hate you."

Val began to cry. She felt vulnerable and exposed, standing outside crying, even though the fence kept the world from seeing her weep, and Kit no longer cared what she did, how she felt.

"Stop it," Val said. "Do you have any idea of what I've been through this week? Do you have any idea what I'm feeling?"

"I don't even care," Kit said. "No, that isn't true. I do care, but it's just force of habit. When you spend sixteen years caring, it's kind of hard to stop."

Val continued to cry. She realized she expected Kit to find a packet of tissues and hand them to her. Kit always carried the tissues. Only Kit wasn't even looking. So she picked up her pocketbook and searched herself. She couldn't find any.

"Here," Kit said, taking some tissues out of her pocket. "Use these."

Val took them and blew her nose. "What's to become of me?" she asked.

"I'm not sure," Kit replied. "But I think it's up to you."

Val nodded. "I wish it weren't," she said. "I liked it better with the lies. It was easier then."

"I liked it better then too," Kit said.

Val wiped away her tears and took a deep breath. "How are things with you and Jamey?" she asked. "Did you go to the play together?"

Kit shook her head. "I went with Malcolm after all," she said. "Pop spent the day wiping Rick's tears."

"I'm sorry," Val said.

"It wasn't your fault," Kit replied. "Besides, there was something I wanted to talk to Malcolm about. An idea I had."

"Can I ask what?" Val said.

Kit laughed. "Of course you can ask," she said. "I may hate you, but that doesn't mean we're not best friends. I wanted to know if there were any colleges that took you a year before graduating. Malcolm said there were, that there was a kid in his high school class who skipped senior year and went right into college instead. He said he was sure I could handle it academically, and he thought it would be the best thing possible for me emotionally. I really love Malcolm. It's like having a sane version of Kevin around."

Val knew she didn't want Kit to go, knew that Kit wouldn't be allowed to if Rick told Jamey to forbid it. For a single blazing moment she hated Kit for deserting her as much as she'd hated Michelle for telling her the truth. She wanted to strike Kit, as she'd struck Michelle, but she held herself back. She'd learned other ways of getting what she wanted from her father. She knew better than to hit.

Kit seemed oblivious to Val's fury. "I love the idea of leaving," she declared. "But I still have this year to get through. And I'm not sure Pop and Mother could survive if I weren't around. I don't know. Maybe this clinic is the answer for Mother. Maybe Pop'll quit his job, become a Legal Services lawyer. I've decided to paint my bedroom ashes of roses. Maybe I'll like it so much I won't want to leave." She smiled at Val.

Val looked at her friend and really saw her for the first time. Force of habit, she thought. And then she remembered what Sister Gina Marie had said about shaking up the pieces, changing the pattern. "If it's important to you to go, I'll talk to Daddy," she said, knowing that was the only gift remaining she could offer to Kit.

"You would?" Kit asked. "You would do that?"

Val nodded.

"But who'll look after you?" Kit asked. "If I'm not around."

"Lots of people," Val said. "I have family." She laughed. "I have family up the kazoo it seems."

"That's right," Kit said. "What was it like? Do you have brothers and sisters now?"

"Thousands of them," Val replied. "I met one." She paused for a moment, knowing she should tell Kit, knowing she would have without even thinking about it the week before. "A sister," she said. "Older than me. Well, they're all older than me. I have another sister who goes to Marymount and three older brothers too."

"Wow," Kit said. "When you stop being an only child, you go all the way."

"Daddy's been giving them money all along," Val said. "Whatever they have, it's because of him. Carmela, my mother, said I've been supporting them. It makes me feel dirty somehow, like I've been selling myself, but I haven't even known it. Does that make sense?"

"Not really," Kit said. "But I know the feeling."

"I don't know who I am anymore," Val said. "I'm not asking you to tell me. I'm just telling you I don't know. Today at school, I had the strangest feeling. I was sitting in French class, and it was like there was a mile of distance between myself and my clothes. Does that make any sense?"

"Not in the slightest," Kit replied.

"I didn't think it would," Val said. "I wanted you to be there, so I could tell you how I felt. I'm sorry. I'm doing it again, aren't I, wanting you just for my sake."

"Don't apologize," Kit said. "I've made it a point of being there for you. And even if I hadn't, after the week you've been through, of course you'd want your friends around."

"Not just any friends," Val said. "You."

"I know," Kit said. "I wanted you home this weekend just so I could explain to someone how much I hated you. You were the only person I know who would have understood."

Val looked around. "I hate these trees," she said. "I think I've always hated them."

"You do?" Kit said. "I always wanted them. I thought it must be great to have a house no one could look into."

Val laughed. "Maybe we should swap places," she said. "If I'm not Val Castaladi anymore, I could be Kit Farrell. And there's no reason why you can't be me."

"I'm Irish," Kit said. "Remember?"

"We'll dye your hair," Val said. "And give you brown contact lenses. Think of all those cousins you could have."

"I have Malcolm," Kit said. "That's enough for right now. Did you like her? Your sister, I mean. The one you met."

"I liked her a lot," Val said. "I don't know how much we have in common, but she was honest with me, and that was a nice change of pace. People keep telling me just as much of the truth as they want, but she told me everything. I appreciated that. I seem to like honesty now, or at least I need it." She smiled. "I even like it in you," she said. "Or I think I will when I stop feeling sorry for myself."

"You've never been self-pitying," Kit said. "Not even that much when your mother was dying."

"That's because I thought Daddy would make things better," Val said. "Now I've lost that. That's the thing I've lost the most. That, and you."

"I'm sorry," Kit said. "I wish this week had never happened. I wish we could go back."

Val nodded. "Will you be in school tomorrow?" she asked.

"Yeah," Kit said. "Pop didn't know I cut today. He didn't come home last night. But he'll probably show up tonight, so I won't be able to get away with anything."

"I wish," Val said, and she began to cry again.

"What?" Kit asked. "What do you wish for?"

"I wish Mama was alive," Val cried, and she sank onto the ground, and let the heaving sobs control her.

Kit knelt down beside her. "It's okay," she said. "We all wish for the impossible all the time." She embraced her friend and let Val weep.

Val found the remains of the tissues. "I'm a mess," she said, getting up. She brushed some leaves off her skirt.

"You're okay," Kit said. She began to help Val clean off her skirt, but Val pulled away.

"I can take care of myself," Val said. "You don't have to keep doing for me."

Kit nodded. "There's a lot to learn," she said. "I haven't gotten it all figured out yet."

"You will," Val said. "Probably a lot faster than me."

"I'll see you in school tomorrow?" Kit said.

"Sure," Val said. "We're having a quiz in chemistry."

"Thanks for the warning," Kit said. "I'd better start studying right away." She looked at Val for a moment, then hugged her. "It'll be okay," she said. "No matter how it ends up."

Val nodded.

Kit started walking away, and then she began to sprint. Val watched as she ran to the gate, opened it, then continued her run. She wondered what that was like, to be able to run with nobody watching, nobody protecting, but then she remembered what Kit was running to, and she knew that sort of freedom came with its own high price.

She brushed herself off some more, and gathered her books and bags together. The sun would be setting soon, and the Indian summer day was turning cold. Val turned away from the evergreens and walked to the front door. Before she had the chance to put her key in the lock, her father opened the door for her.

"Valentina," he said, and Val nodded. As she let him lead her back into his house, she could feel the background shifting.

ABOUT THE AUTHOR

SUSAN BETH PFEFFER graduated from New York University with a degree in television, motion pictures, and radio studies. She is the author of the highly praised *The Year Without Michael*, which was an ALA Best Book for Young Adults and a *Publishers Weekly* Best Book of the Year, as well as The Sebastian Sisters quintet: *Evvie at Sixteen, Thea at Sixteen, Claire at Sixteen, Sybil at Sixteen*, and *Meg at Sixteen*. Susan Beth Pfeffer is a native New Yorker who currently resides in Middletown, New York.